P9-BBO-784

Geronimo Stilton

Thea Stilton

THE SECRET OF THE CRYSTAL FAIRIES

Scholastic Inc.

Published by Scholastic Inc., *Publishers since 1920,* 557 Broadway, New York, NY 10012. SCHOLASTIC and associated logos are trademarks and/or registered trademarks of Scholastic Inc.

Library of Congress Cataloging-in-Publication Data available

ISBN 978-1-338-26859-1

Text by Thea Stilton
Original title *Il segreto delle fate dei cristalli*
Cover by Iacopo Bruno, Giuseppe Facciotto, Barbara Pellizzari, and Flavio Ferron
Illustrations by Giuseppe Facciotto, Chiara Balleello, Barbara Pellizzari, Valeria Brambilla, and Alessandro Muscillo
Graphics by Marta Lorini

Special thanks to AnnMarie Anderson
Translated by Anna Pizzelli
Interior design by Becky James

10 9 8 7 6 5 4 3 2 1 18 19 20 21 22

Printed in China 38

First edition, October 2018

The Thea Sisters
THEA
PAULINA
Colette
Violet
Nicky
PAMELA

The Crystal Kingdom

Welcome to the Crystal Kingdom, home of the Crystal Fairies! This precious, glowing world is inhabited by mysterious and enchanting creatures.

Tourmaline is the queen of the Crystal Kingdom. She is a fair and peaceful ruler who cares deeply for her subjects. She is currently in a deep sleep thanks to an evil spell, and no one has been able to wake her.

Emerald Forest Fairies are gentle creatures who live in the woods. The powerful, rare effervescent emeralds help them protect their beloved forest.

The Knights of Crystal Rock are loyal, brave knights who protect the Crystal Kingdom from danger.

Dark Fairies are mysterious fairies who live underground. They are experts in working with metal and precious stones.

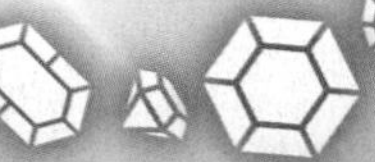

Ruby Fairies are generous creatures who live in an intricate web of caves. They are the only ones who know how to get around in this maze without getting lost.

Golden Elves are wise elves who live in the magical Eternal Woods, where they loyally guard its many secrets.

Diamond is a brave knight in search of his beloved, a fairy named Esmeralda. They are both under the same evil spell.

Esmeralda is a gentle fairy who is trapped by the same evil spell as Diamond. If the Thea Sisters can break the spell, she will be an invaluable guide as they travel through the Crystal Kingdom.

Fang is a wise and courageous wolf who is the protector of the shining Jade Jungle.

Selenite is the keeper and protector of the most precious stone in the whole kingdom: the Sweet Awakening Gem!

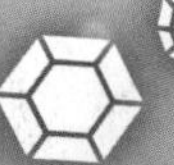

VACATION TIME!

A warm, gentle ocean breeze blew through the open window, bringing the pleasant scent of flowers and summer with it.

"It's such a beautiful day," Nicky said with a sigh as she looked longingly out the window. "We should pack a picnic lunch and head to the beach!"

Her friends Pamela and Violet smiled. Exams were done and the sun was shining high in the sky. From their window, they could see the turquoise sparkle of the inviting water that surrounded Whale Island. They knew how much Nicky loved being outdoors, and they were about to agree to the outing when Colette squeaked.

"I don't know," Colette said grumpily. "It's so hot today I can't bear the thought of my fur being covered in sand. I can't wait for my trip to the French Riviera. It's sunny there, but the air is cool, and there are so many fabumouse boutiques!"

Right then Paulina walked into the room.

"I finally did it, Nicky!" she squeaked enthusiastically. "I booked the tickets for our trip to the Galapagos Islands!"

"Woo-hoo!" Nicky replied happily.

Colette stared at her friends.

"Are you two sure you really want to spend your summer with all those lizards?" she asked.

"Absolutely!" came Paulina's reply. "The Galapagos is one of the most diverse areas in the whole world. There are so many different varieties of plant and animal life."

Amazing!
It's so hot!
I have the tickets!

"Be sure to take a lot of pictures," Violet reminded them. "It's going to be an amazing trip."

"Of course," Paulina agreed. "And you'd better send us updates from yours."

Violet and her parents were about to embark on a trip across Europe by train!

"Definitely," Violet agreed. "My parents and I have been planning this trip for a long time. I'm really excited!"

"I just know our summer VACATIONS will be amazing," Pamela said. She was heading home to New York City to spend time with her family.

"I only wish we could travel together," Violet said. "I'll miss you all!"

"Me, too!" Colette said, hugging her. "But we'll MouseTime whenever we can."

"Let's take a picture together before we all

head off to different parts of the world," Paulina suggested.

"Good idea," the friends agreed, smiling for the camera.

CLICK!

"Too bad Thea isn't here," Colette said. "She usually stops by **MOUSEFORD** before summer vacation begins."

"But just think of where she is right now,"

Nicky said, sighing. "She's so lucky that she had the chance to join an international scientific expedition to the **Arctic**!"

Just then a phone rang.

RING! RING! RING!

The Thea Sisters all checked their cell phones, but the sound was coming from somewhere else.

"That's Thea's secret cell phone!" Colette said.

It's Thea's phone!

The five mice looked at one another in **SURPRISE**.

"What should we do?" Violet asked.

"We should answer it," Nicky replied confidently.

"Remember what Thea told us after our last

mission? She said she trusts us and thinks we're ready to handle difficult situations **on our own**!"

So Paulina took a small key hanging from her necklace and used it to open a drawer in the table next to the sofa. The **secret cell phone** was hidden there. The screen was flashing: The call was coming from the **SEVEN ROSES UNIT**!

THE SEVEN ROSES UNIT

The headquarters of the Seven Roses Unit is hidden in the icy Arctic. Only the members of the unit know how to find the entrance.

THE ROSE PENDANT

Each researcher has a pendant that contains their personal information. It can be used as a key to open doors in the unit headquarters.

The Hall of the Seven Roses

In the heart of the unit is the Hall of the Seven Roses. It is a living map that shows every Fantasy World and reports on each one's condition. When a world is in danger, a crack appears in the map.

The Crystal Elevator

A glass elevator is the gateway to the imaginary kingdoms. Only Will Mystery can operate the elevator using a special keyboard and a secret combination of musical notes. Then the power of music transports its occupants to a fantasy world!

A NEW MISSION

Will Mystery is the director of the Seven Roses Unit, a supersecret research center that studies fantasy worlds inhabited by characters from fables and legends.

As soon as the Thea Sisters answered the phone, **Will Mystery** appeared on the screen.

"Hello, mouselets," the director said. "How are you?"

"Hi. We're great!" Paulina replied. "Our **classes** just ended, and we're about to go on **VACATION**."

"Thea already left on an expedition to the **North Pole**," Violet

explained quickly. "That's why we answered her phone."

"Yes, I know," Will replied. "I've already spoken with Thea by satellite phone, and I know about her trip. I need help, and since Thea can't get here, I'm calling on you. Thea and I agree that you five mice have become expert agents, and I **trust** you completely!"

"Thank you, Will!" Colette replied. Will's trust was extremely important to her and her friends.

"Which of the kingdoms is in **DANGER**?" Pam asked seriously.

The Thea Sisters were well aware of all the treasures and wonders of the **imaginary kingdoms**, and the thought that one of them was in trouble was upsetting.

"It's the **CRYSTAL KINGDOM**, home of the **Crystal Fairies**," Will replied.

"And I'm afraid it's quite **SERIOUS**."

"The name itself gives you an idea of how delicate the Crystal Kingdom must be," Violet remarked.

"You're right," Will said, nodding. "It's an extremely fragile and precious land. "I know you're all about to leave on your

vacations, and I'm sorry to ruin your plans, but I really need **HELP**."

"Holey cheese, our vacations can wait!" Pam exclaimed.

"Yes, of course we'll come," Colette added. "We're **SPECIAL AGENTS**, and our duty is to protect the imaginary kingdoms."

"Thank you, mouselets!" Will said, a look of relief on his snout. "I knew I could count on you!"

"Should we take the **SUPERSONIC HELICOPTER**?" Nicky asked.

"Yes," Will replied. "The pilot will pick you up on the beach at **midnight**. Make sure nobody sees you."

"No problem," Colette replied.

"I'll see you later at headquarters. Have a safe flight!" Will said.

"**Scurry up** and pack, mouselets," Violet

reminded her friends. "We don't have much time!"

Back in their room, Paulina and Nicky traded their snorkels and swimsuits for sturdy shoes and warm layers of clothing.

Meanwhile, Violet **texted** her parents to let them know that they would have to begin their trip without her!

In their bedroom, Pamela and Colette were busy stuffing their backpacks for the mission.

Pam noticed Colette stash **three packets** of pink tissues in her bag.

"What?"

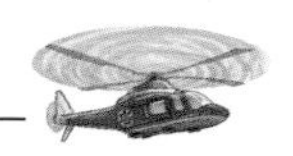

Colette asked, blushing. “Why are you looking at me like that? They could be useful!”

“They’re **pink**, Coco,” her friend remarked, grinning.

“Exactly,” Colette replied. “That means they’re **very chic**! I may not be able to spend my vacation stocking up on new fashions on the French Riviera, but that doesn’t mean I can’t be *stylish*!”

Pam burst out laughing. Her roommate would never change!

The hours went by quickly, and soon it was time for the Thea Sisters to meet the helicopter on the **beach**. They quickly scurried across the dark, deserted campus, making it just in time. Right after they stepped onto the moonlit stretch of sand, a light appeared in the **BLACK** sky. As they watched, the light slowly grew closer.

"It looks like a shooting star," Violet whispered.

The helicopter landed smoothly, and the mouselets got on. Moments later they were on their way to the **SEVEN ROSES UNIT**!

THE OPAL'S MESSAGE

In the DARKNESS of the icy cold night, the supersonic helicopter sped toward the huge ICEBERG that was the secret gateway to the Seven Roses Unit.

As the helicopter approached the ice, the Thea Sisters gasped. In the moonlight, the smooth, shiny surface was a deep **BLUE** color.

"It looks like a precious stone glittering in the middle of the ocean!" Colette exclaimed.

At these words, the Thea Sisters were reminded of the CRYSTAL KINGDOM and the mission ahead.

Then the pilot pushed a **button** and the

iceberg split in half, revealing the gateway. The helicopter flew inside and the pilot deftly maneuvered through a **tunnel** that led to the Seven Roses Unit entrance.

When the Thea Sisters set paw on the landing strip, **Will Mystery** was there to meet them.

"I'm so glad you're here." He welcomed them with a smile.

"You seemed pretty *worried* when you called," Paulina said.

"You're right," he explained, leading them inside. "I received a request for help directly from the Crystal Fairies."

"That must mean the situation is very **SERIOUS**!" Nicky exclaimed.

"I'm afraid so," Will said gravely. "Come with me and I'll explain everything."

He led them to the Hall of the Seven Roses

and the **living map**. Will pointed out the Crystal Kingdom. A large **CRACK** in the map ran through the center of the kingdom, dividing it in half. This was a clear sign that something was very, very **wrong**.

Next to the crack on the map was a strange, **glowing** object.

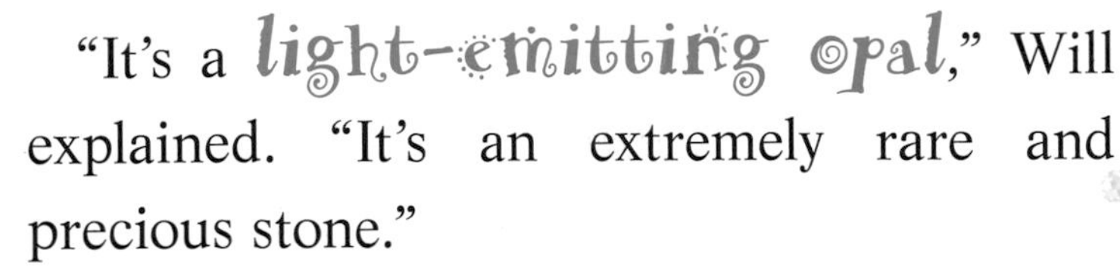

"It's a light-emitting opal," Will explained. "It's an extremely rare and precious stone."

"Does it come from the Crystal Kingdom?" Paulina asked.

"Yes," Will said. "The Crystal Fairies sent it to us along

with their request for HELP!"

The Thea Sisters studied the stone.

"How does it work?" Paulina asked.

"The opal changes COLOR depending on the message it wants to convey," Will explained.

Violet looked at it closely. "It looks **red** right now," she remarked.

"The color isn't very bright, though," Colette said. "It looks faded."

"Red means DANGER," Will explained. "And faded red is definitely not a good sign."

"Something TERRIBLE is going on, isn't it?" Pam asked.

"Look here," Will replied, pointing at the crack on the map of the Crystal Kingdom. "Can you see how **deep** it is?"

"Oh no!" Colette exclaimed.

"There's something else here," Paulina pointed out. "It looks like a dark ring."

Will sighed.

"It's right in the center — around the kingdom's **heart**," Colette whispered, worried.

"Come on, let's go," Will said quickly. "We have no time to waste."

THE SEVEN ROSES UNIT

1. Landing platform
2. Elevator
3. Access to the surface
4. Hall of the Seven Roses
5. Supercomputer room
6. Relaxation area
7. Research laboratory
8. Clothing and supply room

THE CRYSTAL KINGDOM

When the mouselets walked into the room, the supercomputer was already on.

"The Crystal Kingdom is very far away and the least known kingdom," Will explained. "Because of this, we really need the light-emitting opal." He placed the stone in a special GLASS CONTAINER connected to the computer.

"Is this a new machine?" Paulina asked, curious.

"Yes, the IT department just finished setting it up a few days ago," Will replied. "It is fitted with a special scanner that analyzes objects and transmits information to the computer."

"So when the computer analyzes this stone, it will provide us with **DATA** about the Crystal Kingdom?" Paulina asked.

"Yes. If it's working as it should," Will replied.

After a moment, the computer screen **LIT UP** with information on the mysterious kingdom.

THE CRYSTAL KINGDOM

POPULATION: Fairies, elves, trolls, and other precious creatures live here.

IMPORTANT INFORMATION: The **Crystal Fairies** are the kingdom's guardians. They are also expert goldsmiths and specialists in precious stones. They know all the secret properties and uses for each precious stone and mineral.

LEADER: The ruler of the Crystal Kingdom is the kind and selfless **Queen Tourmaline**. She became queen at a young age thanks to her loyal tutor and friend, Calcedonio.

HISTORY: Queen Tourmaline's parents fought a hard-won war against an evil wizard who wanted to conquer their kingdom. Tourmaline was entrusted to **Calcedonio's** care, and he became her teacher and friend. Before leaving the kingdom, Calcedonio told Queen Tourmaline that her royal scepter holds a hidden, mysterious secret.

JOYSTONE CASTLE: The queen's palace is nestled in a verdant valley, surrounded by **crystal gardens** and **quartz walls** that prevent unwanted guests from wandering in.

ENTRANCE: Located on a small island in the **Sapphire Sea**.

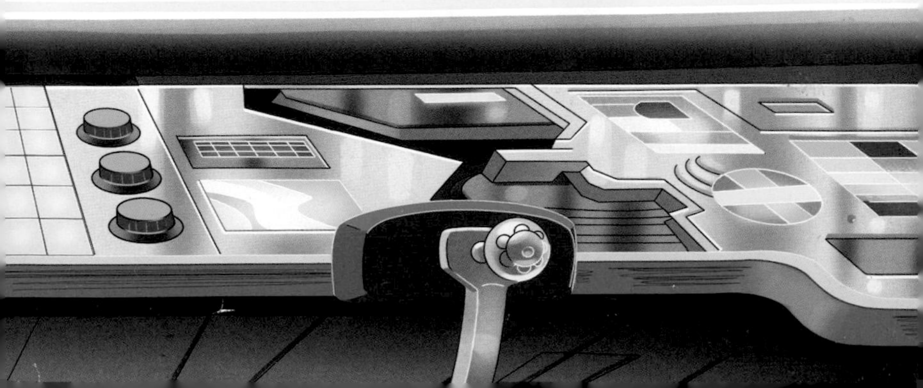

The mouselets looked at one another, excited. Will Mystery grabbed a backpack and put the light-emitting opal inside. Then he led the mouselets toward the crystal elevator.

"Will the elevator take us to the island in the Sapphire Sea?" Nicky asked.

"Yes," Will replied. "When we get to the Crystal Kingdom, we'll have to figure out how to get to Joystone Castle."

Once they were all inside the elevator, Will played a series of notes on the magic keyboard. A sweet melody filled the air as the Thea Sisters held paws expectantly:

A NEW ADVENTURE WAS ABOUT TO BEGIN!

To a new adventure!
Are you ready?
Yes! Let's go!

A MYSTERIOUS ISLAND

When the mice exited the elevator, they found themselves in a thick forest of palm trees.

"It doesn't seem like this gateway to the CRYSTAL KINGDOM gets much use," Nicky remarked as she and the other Thea Sisters followed Will Mystery through a tangle of branches.

Finally, they emerged from the trees and found themselves on a beautiful sandy beach.

"Wow, what an amazing view!" Colette exclaimed.

"The light is truly incredible," Paulina remarked.

"This island doesn't seem very big," Colette said. "It shouldn't be too hard to find the entrance to the Crystal Kingdom — and the way to Joystone Castle."

"Let's start looking," Will suggested.

So the mouselets split up and began EXPLORING the island. Nicky and Pam headed in one direction, while Violet and Colette headed in another. Meanwhile, Will and Paulina explored the beach.

Later, the mice met up back at the beach, confused expressions on their snouts.

"We didn't find anything," Nicky said.

"Neither did we," Violet replied.

"It looks like all there is around us is the sparkling sea," Paulina said thoughtfully.

"The middle of the island is completely covered by forest," Pam pointed out. "We searched, but there are no passageways."

"It's very strange," Will agreed. "Why aren't there any visible paths to follow?"

"Will, what if the path is through the **water**?" Paulina said suddenly.

"That's an idea!" Will said, excited. "We are surrounded by the sea, after all!" He

walked toward the shore.

Paulina followed, dipping her paw into the surf.

"It's warm!" she exclaimed. "And so clear. It looks like a swimming pool!"

Will **smiled**. "Maybe if we just walk out

into the water, the passageway will become clear," he suggested.

Will stepped into the surf and waded **deeper** into the water. Suddenly, a school of threatening-looking SILVER fish surrounded him.

"What's happening?" Paulina asked.

Will took a step backward as the fish came CLOSER and CLOSER.

"It looks like these fish are trying to keep us away from something!" he said.

"Let's get back to the beach," Paulina said nervously. Will grabbed her paw, and they walked back together.

"Is something wrong?" Colette asked as the pair returned to the soft, sandy beach.

"There are some **FIERCE-LOOKING** silver fish in the water," Paulina explained. "They won't let us pass."

"So what do we do now?" Violet asked.

The THEA SISTERS and Will looked at one another, wondering.

Finally, Nicky squeaked.

"It looks like we're stuck here!"

THE WAVY PATH

The Thea Sisters and Will stared at the sparkling sea in front of them, hoping to come up with a plan.

"We looked everywhere for an entrance to the Crystal Kingdom," Violet mused thoughtfully. "Why can't we find it?"

"The Crystal Fairies asked for our help," Will said. "I don't think they would leave us

here with no way into the kingdom."

At that moment, Colette noticed a shiny spot in the waves.

"LOOK!" she said, pointing at the sea.

"It's just a reflection off the water," Violet replied distractedly.

"No, it's moving!" Colette exclaimed.

The mice scrambled to their paws and watched in disbelief as the shiny SPOT grew closer and closer. Then, suddenly, the spot JUMPED up in the sky.

"It's a fish!" Paulina cried, stunned.

Will took two steps back, thinking of the THREATENING silver fish they had just encountered.

"Maybe we should move away from the shore," Will suggested.

"Do not be afraid!" the fish said in a mysterious, musical voice.

"**HOLEY CHEESE!**" Pamela exclaimed. "Is it talking to us? What should we do?"

Will took a few hesitant steps toward the fish, followed by the Thea Sisters.

"**Welcome**," the fish greeted them, bowing deeply.

"Hello," Will replied. "Did you know about our arrival?"

"Yes, of course!" the fish replied, sounding a little **insulted**. "I was sent here to take you to the **mainland**. The Crystal Fairies are waiting there for you!"

"Oh, great!" Colette exclaimed. "We'll be at the castle soon, then."

"I am *Turquoise*, guardian of the **Wavy Path**," the fish continued.

"The Wavy Path?" Paulina repeated.

"It's a hidden path to the Crystal Kingdom,

made of precious marine sapphires," he explained.

"So there *is* a passageway from here to the Crystal Kingdom!" Pamela exclaimed.

"Of course there is!" Turquoise replied.

"But it's **impossible** to find unless you know where to **LOOK**. Now, we'd better go: The fairies can't wait to meet you! "Walk in a **single** line right behind me."

The mouselets looked at one another, unsure whether to trust the **strange** fish.

"Well, here goes!" Pam said as she **boldly** stepped forward. Will and the other Thea Sisters followed. Sure enough, a solid path formed beneath their paws as they moved through the water.

"The marine sapphires form an **UNDERWATER** walkway that can't be seen from above the surface," Colette said.

"They're so **beautiful**!" Nicky said, mesmerized.

"Is this the **Wavy Path**?" Paulina asked.

"Yes," Turquoise replied. "Follow the path all the way to the mainland. Proceed with

CAUTION and **CONFIDENCE**, and nothing bad will happen to you."

"What about you?" Violet asked, worried. "Aren't you going with us?"

"I'll go with you until the end of the path," Turquoise explained, "but when you reach the mainland, you will meet a new guide."

"**Thank you!**" the mouselets exclaimed.

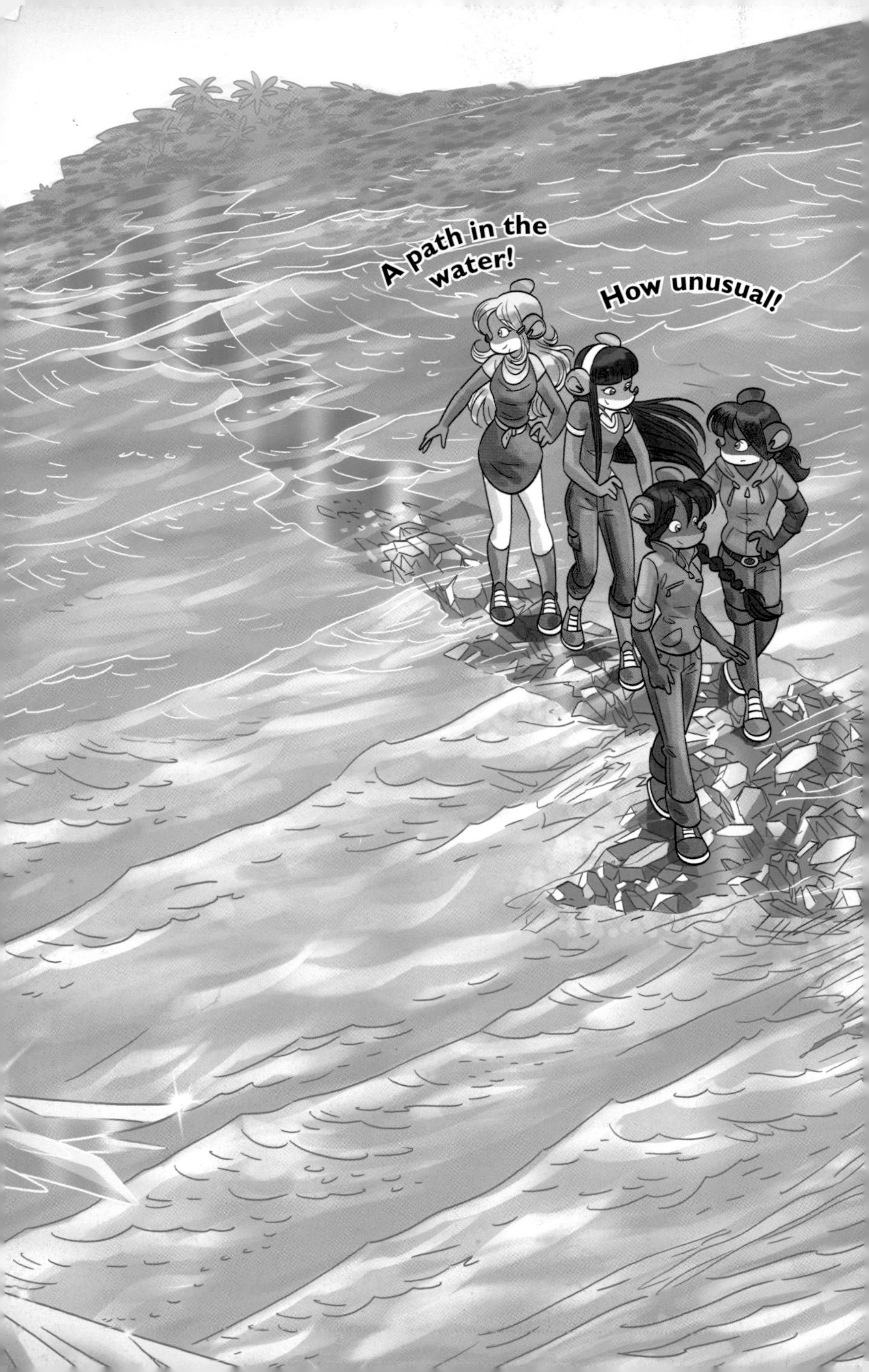
A path in the water!
How unusual!

This way!
Cool!

A WHIRLPOOL IN THE WAVES

The Thea Sisters and Will walked in a single-file line along the Wavy Path, Turquoise swimming along beside them.

As she walked, Nicky studied the sparkling water around her.

"It looks like there's a strong ***current*** in this part of the sea," she remarked.

"That current leads directly to the **STONE OF THE DEEP**," Turquoise explained.

"It is the largest precious stone in the Sapphire Sea, and it's found in the deepest part

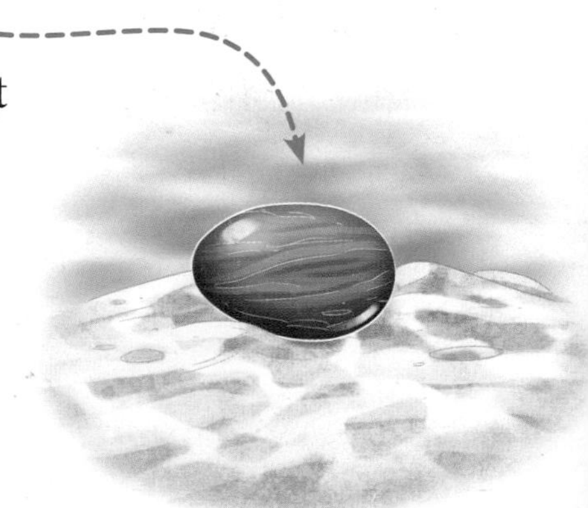

of the ocean. The sea creatures that live nearby say the ocean waves originate from and return to the **STONE OF THE DEEP**, taking with them everything they find on their way."

Suddenly, there was a **SCREAM** followed by a **splash**.

"**HELP!**" Violet cried.

Colette had been walking right behind her friend and tried to grab her when she slipped off the sapphire path.

"Vi!" Colette shouted.

"**Will, we have to do something!**" Paulina called out in alarm.

"I'm jumping in," he declared.

"Wait, don't!" Turquoise said, stopping him. "It's too dangerous and you won't be able to reach her. The ***current*** in this part of the sea is too strong."

"But we can't just leave her!" Colette cried as she watched Violet drift farther away.

"The waves will take her all the way to the Stone of the Deep!" Nicky added, terrified.

Colette turned toward the fish.

"We have to help our FRIEND, Turquoise," she said firmly. "Please, there must be something we can do!"

"I cannot leave the path," the guardian fish replied. "But I can ask the Current Carnelians to help. They are the only creatures in the Crystal Kingdom who can swim in the Sapphire Sea current."

"QUICK, DON'T WASTE ANOTHER MINUTE!" Will urged the fish.

With a jump, Turquoise dove underwater. The Thea Sisters and Will held their breath as they waited for the fish to resurface. Minutes went by with no sign of Turquoise.

Finally, Will couldn't take it any longer.

"Wait for me here!" he exclaimed.

Then, before the mouselets could stop him, he JUMPED in.

They watched as their friend tossed and turned in the waves. A second later, though, something incredible happened: A school of shiny red fish lifted Will up. It was the Current Carnelians, carrying him safely through the rough waves.

"Thank you, my friends," Will said with relief as soon as the fish swam to his RESCUE.

The tiny creatures carried Will through the current, floating on the waves.

"Violet!" Will shouted "Violet!"

Suddenly, the waves became bigger and Will saw a gigantic whirlpool right in front of him. He was getting closer to the STONE OF THE DEEP!

Then Will saw Violet in the waves ahead:

The current was about to sweep her into the **whirlpool**!

Luckily, Will got to her just in time. With the help of the Carnelians, he managed to grab her by her paw and pull her to safety.

"Are you okay?" Will asked.

"Now I am," Violet said, relief in her voice. "Thank you for saving me!"

"It wasn't just me," Will explained. "The **Carnelians** helped! Now, let's get back to the others. They must be waiting for us."

The **Current Carnelians** guided Violet and Will directly to the mainland at the end of the Wavy Path. The Thea Sisters were standing on the shore, waiting for them, and *Turquoise* splashed in the water nearby.

"Thank goodmouse you're both okay!" the mouselets cried as they surrounded them. They hugged Violet very tightly.

"It was all thanks to the Current Carnelians," Will explained. "**Thank you, my friends!**"

The little red fish waved good-bye with their fins and quickly swam away.

"And thank you, too, Turquoise!" the mouselets said.

"It was a great honor to assist you," the

fish said with a smile.

And with a **swift** flap of his fin, he returned to his post as guardian of the underwater path.

THE EMERALD FOREST

Now that they were on dry land again, Will and the Thea Sisters were ready to continue their journey to **Joystone Castle**. They waited patiently for the guide Turquoise said would meet them there.

After a few minutes, they finally heard something.

"**GREETINGS, MY FRIENDS!**" called a sweet voice.

They turned to find a most beautiful fairy staring at them with glimmering green eyes.

"Good morning!" Colette replied.

"My name is Silvis, and I am an Emerald Forest fairy," she explained. "I am here to escort you. You are expected at Joystone Castle."

She fluttered along, leading the way through an incredible forest.

"This seems like a magical place," Nicky remarked as she and her friends followed the fairy.

"Yes," Silvis confirmed. "Here the fairies live in complete **HARMONY** with nature. Do you hear that? It's the sound of an emerald bird, brightening our day with its chirping."

"What a beautiful song!" Violet exclaimed.

"Unfortunately, our forest and the entire Crystal Kingdom is under threat," the fairy continued, her voice worried.

"We know," Will explained. "That's the reason we're here. We want to HELP!"

"Do you know where the threat is coming from?" Paulina asked.

The fairy's wings stopped fluttering, and she turned to look at them.

"A dragon," she said gravely.

"A dragon?!" Nicky cried, surprised.

"Yes," Silvis said sadly. "A terrible dragon has been turning our precious stones into rocks and ashes with his FIERY BREATH."

"That's terrible!" Colette exclaimed.

Silvis nodded.

"And that's not all," she said. "Every time the dragon attacks us, he becomes BIGGER and STRONGER. It's as if destroying the Crystal Kingdom empowers him!"

"Look over there," Nicky said, pointing to a tree. "The emerald trees have turned to gray rocks!"

"Now I understand why your queen sent for us," Will said sadly.

"It wasn't Queen Tourmaline who sent for you — it was the rest of the fairies! You see, there is more to the story," the fairy said.

The Thea Sisters listened as Silvis told her tale.

"Some time ago, our beloved Queen Tourmaline fell into a deep sleep," she explained, tears glistening in her eyes.

"No one knows why, and no one has been able to WAKE her."

"Oh no!" Violet exclaimed.

"All the fairies are very grateful you have come to our rescue," Silvis continued. "Together we hope to be able to stop the dragon and wake **Queen Tourmaline** before it's too late."

A moment later, a second fairy appeared behind a bush, looking very worried.

"Silvis, quick!" she said. "The dragon

is destroying the east side of the forest! We need your help!"

"**We're coming with you!**" Will said.

Then the fairies led the way through the forest, Will and the Thea Sisters racing after them.

A BLAZING ATTACK

When Will, the Thea Sisters, and the fairies got to the east side of the forest, they found a **terrible** sight: An entire grove of trees had been **SCORCHED** and turned to dust and rocks.

"We have to do something!" Nicky exclaimed.

Two more fairies with downcast looks on their faces joined them.

"Unfortunately, there is no way to stop him," one fairy explained. "Our **arrows** bounce off the dragon's armored body."

"If we can't fight him, we'll have to **outsmart** him," Paulina suggested.

"We could try to **CAPTURE** him," Paulina

said suddenly, a determined look on her snout.

"Paulina's right," Nicky agreed. "We could build a trap out of **leaves** and **branches**."

"Great idea!" Silvis said eagerly. "The branches that didn't burn are

very STRONG. I'm certain we can build something that will work!"

"Let's get started, then!" Will declared.

He and the Thea Sisters quickly built a NET that they positioned between two LARGE trees.

"But how will we LURE the dragon into the trap?" Violet asked.

Silvis pointed to the EMERALD on her forehead. "By showing him something he wants," she explained. "This emerald is extremely rare. It's an effervescent emerald — see the BUBBLES on the surface?

"They are only found in this forest, and they are its purest and most POWERFUL essence."

"Only the fairies can wear them because they come from the most secret place in the forest," the second fairy explained. "We

guard the spot at **all times**."

"The dragon will find the effervescent emerald *alluring*," Silvis went on. "We can use it to lead him right into the **TRAP**! We can't let him destroy any more of the Emerald Forest."

"I agree," said Will. Then he and the **THEA SISTERS** hid in the trees behind the trap, ready for **ACTION**.

The fairies flew off to find the dragon, and Silvis made sure her **EFFERVESCENT EMERALD** was shining brightly. It didn't take long for the dragon to spot the sparkling stone. He was quickly drawn in by the emerald's enchanting **twinkle**.

As the Thea Sisters watched, they saw the dragon's shiny **golden** armor and his ***FIERY*** eyes as he flew closer and closer to Silvis.

The dragon had been moving *cautiously*, but as soon as he saw the emerald, he swooped forward and tried to grab the fairy.

The Thea Sisters quickly released the trap, and the net sprang up, trapping the dragon inside the **woven** branches!

The dragon began to thrash around inside the net, **huffing** and **puffing** angrily. In

no time, the heat from his ***FIERY*** breath had burned through the branches, and the dragon was free.

"No!" Colette gasped.

"Remember what the fairies said," Paulina reminded her friend. "Every time the dragon attacks, he grows **STRONGER**!"

In the meantime, a smoky cloud began enveloping the forest.

"Watch out!" Violet cried as the haze moved toward Silvis and her fairy friends.

Unfortunately, one of the fairies was unable to fly away quickly enough. The THICK, dark smoke enveloped her, and she fell to the ground, unconscious.

"Eliane!" Silvis called out in dismay.

Will and the Thea Sisters ran to help the fallen fairy while Silvis challenged the dragon.

"What did you do to her?" she cried, her eyes FLASHING. "Coward! Go pick on creatures your own size!"

Upon hearing those words, the dragon stopped as though frozen. He looked at Eliane, then at Silvis.

Then, suddenly, something inexplicable

happened: Instead of attacking the fairy, the dragon turned around and **flew away**.

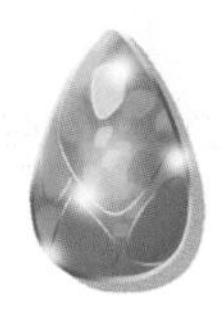

JOYSTONE CASTLE

As the dragon flew off, Silvis returned to her friends. Eliane was still lying on the ground, eyes closed, looking pale.

"She isn't waking up," Violet said, worried.

Silvis put her hand on Eliane's forehead, looked at the two other fairies, and quietly nodded at them. Then the fairies all placed one hand on the EFFERVESCENT EMERALD each was wearing, and the other hand on Eliane's forehead.

Finally, after what seemed like a long time, Eliane opened her EYES.

"You did it!" Violet said joyfully as she looked at the fairies in disbelief.

"It's the power of the EFFERVESCENT

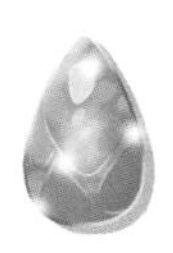

EMERALDS," Silvis explained.

"And the power of your *friendship*!" Colette added. The mouselet and fairy exchanged a knowing smile.

Silvis bid farewell to her fairy friends and continued on the JOURNEY to Joystone Castle with Will and the Thea Sisters.

"What happened back there when you

faced the dragon?" Paulina asked as the group moved through the forest.

"I was very **ANGRY** about what had happened to Eliane," Silvis explained. "And I was about to attack the dragon."

She paused and looked down as if she was **ashamed**.

The dragon looked sorry . . .

Really?!

"But then he looked me straight in the eye before he turned and flew away!"

"And why do you think he did that?" Colette asked, confused.

"I don't know," Silvis replied thoughtfully. "He almost looked sorry . . ."

"Really?!" Pam asked, surprised.

"He was looking at Eliane as if he felt RESPONSIBLE for what he had done," Silvis said.

"Why is he trying to DESTROY the Crystal Kingdom?" Nicky asked. "It doesn't make sense."

"True," Will agreed. "It's a real mystery, and I'm sure we'll get to the bottom of it. But right now, we really have to focus on getting to Joystone Castle."

"Your friend is right," Silvis agreed. "This way!"

The fairy led them to the edge of a ROCKY expanse that was dotted with enormouse, pointy quartz crystals.

"This is the ROCKY CRYSTAL PATH," the fairy announced. "It will lead you toward the castle."

"Fascinating!" Nicky murmured as she studied the giant crystals.

"It is," Silvis said with a nod. "But you must be very CAREFUL. The crystals are as TREACHEROUS as they are beautiful."

Will and the mouselets approached the sparkling maze of rocks with caution.

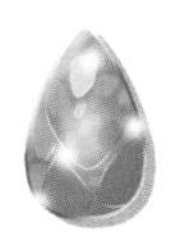

"Holey cheese!" Pam exclaimed. "They are really **GORGEOUS**!"

"How **DANGEROUS** could these remarkable rocks really be?" Colette asked curiously.

"Their surface does not always reflect the real world," the fairy warned. "At times it can be deceiving. The crystals **REFLECT**

and multiply the feelings and fears of those who walk among them, just like a house of **MIRRORS**. If you get scared while looking at all the reflections, your **fear** will only increase. And if you stop and gaze at your reflection for too long, you will want to do nothing but **admire** what you see. Then you'll forget your **MISSION** and become lost in the maze **forever**!"

The mouselets turned to look at Colette.

"**Why are you all looking at me?**" she complained.

The Thea Sisters giggled in reply. They loved their friend dearly, but she could get caught up in her *appearance*!

"You have to be **STRONG**," Silvis went on. "If you follow the road, you have nothing to fear."

"Aren't you coming with us?" Violet asked.

"Unfortunately, I cannot," she replied. "We

fairies cannot **roam** too far from the forest we guard. Once you get through the **ROCK CRYSTALS**, you will reach a fork in the road at the **Blue Topaz**. There you have to trust your instincts: If your choice is correct, the road will turn into **red coral** and you will soon arrive at your destination."

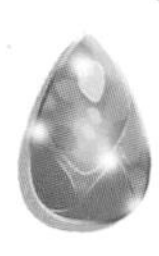

"And what happens if we make the wrong choice?" Paulina asked.

"The path will turn to GRAVEL and ROCK and you will not be able to return to the beginning again."

"Come on, sisters!" Pam exclaimed. "We can do this!"

"If all goes well, you will meet the Lapis Falls Guardian Fairies at the end of the coral path," Silvis said. "They will be your next guides."

"Thank you, Silvis," Will said graciously. "Your help was invaluable."

Silvis nodded and hugged each of them, wishing them well on their MISSION. Then she stood at the edge of the Emerald Forest and waved good-bye.

THE ROCKY CRYSTAL PATH

"It's too bad Silvis can't come with us," Paulina said sadly.

"I know," Will agreed. "But she gave us everything we need to get through the maze."

"Well, yes," Pam remarked. "Though we'll also have to rely on our intuition . . ."

"And our courage!" Colette added.

Violet couldn't help but look at the sparkling stone.

"Oh!" she gasped. "It's so shiny!"

"Stop!" Paulina **WARNED** her. "Don't look at it, Vi! Remember what Silvis told us."

Violet had to struggle to look away, but after a moment, she was able to do it.

From then on, the group of friends walked carefully on the narrow path that ran through the LARGE CRYSTALS that rose from the ground like columns. Will led the way, and Colette was **LAST** in line. The mouselet walked with her paws at the sides of her snout so she wouldn't be tempted to peek at the crystals.

But suddenly, Colette caught a glimpse of her own blonde wavy hair out of the corner of her eye. She stopped walking.

The **REFLECTION** was so shiny in the light of the quartz crystals.

Is that what my hair really looks like? Colette thought as she took a **QUICK GLANCE**. But once she took a peek, she couldn't look away, and soon Colette had become separated from the group.

Meanwhile, the rest of the group continued on, unaware of what had happened.

"These crystals are so **BRIGHT**, it's difficult not to look at them," Paulina remarked.

"You're right," Pam agreed. "But we have to **resist**!"

"It's too bad we can't stop to admire them," Violet said sadly. "They almost look **PINK** in the light, don't they, Colette?"

But there was no reply.

"*Colette?!*" Violet called again.

When she didn't answer a second time, everyone became ALARMED. They realized that their friend was no longer with them.

"Where is she?" Paulina asked.

"I don't know!" Nicky exclaimed, distraught. She had been walking directly in front of her friend. "I was so focused on keeping my eyes off the crystals, I didn't notice anything else."

"It's not your fault," Will said, comforting her.

"What do we do now?" Pam moaned. "It won't be easy to find her in this maze."

What none of them realized was that, in the meantime, Colette had wandered into a **secret tunnel**. When she reached the end of the tunnel, the mouselet looked around, **AMAZED**. In front of her, an impressive Crystal Castle was nestled in the rocks.

Suddenly, Colette heard hooves against the hard rock behind her. She whirled around to find herself facing a knight on a white horse.

"Who are you, and how did you

get here?" he asked **STERNLY**.

"My name is Colette," she replied. "I got lost while I was following the **ROCKY CRYSTAL PATH**."

"My name is **Petrus**," the knight replied. "I am the first horseman of the **Knights of Crystal Rock**."

"Nice to meet you," Colette said. "Is there any way you could help me find my way back. My friends must be looking for me!

"We are on a special mission to help the **CRYSTAL FAIRIES** protect their kingdom and save **Queen Tourmaline**," she explained.

"I know about the dragon and the **THREAT** he poses to our kingdom," he said. "The other knights and I have tried our best to **PROTECT** our corner of the Crystal Kingdom, but I'm afraid we weren't able to **DEFEAT** the dragon. I don't think he'll stop until he

finds what he's looking for!"

"What do you mean?" Colette asked. "What is he **SEARCHING** for?"

"If I only knew," Petrus replied, a faraway look in his eye. "But now I have a chance to make up for failing to stop the dragon. I would be glad to help you return to your friends — and to your **important** mission! It is a knight's sacred duty to help those in need. And now I will lead you back to your friends!"

THE FORK IN THE ROAD

It wasn't long before Colette found herself snout-to-snout with someone familiar again.

"*Nicky?!*" she cried as she emerged from behind a **GIANT** crystal.

"*Colette!*" Nicky replied. "We were

so worried about you!"

"Are you okay?" Violet asked.

"Yes, I'm fine," Colette said. "I'm so sorry I worried you."

"What happened?" Will wanted to know.

So Colette explained how she had stared at her **reflection** for too long and ended up wandering down a tunnel that led to the impressive Crystal Castle.

"Holey cheese!" Paulina cried. "There's a castle in the middle of this maze?"

Colette nodded.

"I couldn't believe it, either," she said. "And I wouldn't know how to find it again . . . it's a **SECRET** location."

Then she told her friends about meeting Petrus and what he had told her about the dragon.

"So he's **LOOKING** for something

specific!" Paulina remarked.

"But we have no idea what that is," Nicky pointed out.

"**We'll find out soon**," Will replied. "I'm sure of it. Now, let's get back on the road."

The group of friends continued their journey, and soon enough they reached a fork in the road.

"There it is, mouselets," Will said. "The **Blue Topaz**!"

The Thea Sisters stared in awe at a gigantic **PURE BLUE** stone. It stood in the middle of the road, sparkling brightly.

"This must be the rock Silvis mentioned," Nicky agreed.

On top of the rock she discovered a small gold needle, like the kind on a **compass**.

"Hmmm," Violet said, studying the topaz.

"Maybe this rock is a giant navigational device."

"I don't think so. It isn't marked with any cardinal points," Colette pointed out. "And remember: Silvis told us to **TRUST OUR INSTINCTS**."

"**LOOK!**" Nicky exclaimed suddenly. "The needle is moving!"

The golden needle spun like a top. When it stopped moving, it was pointing to the **road on the right**.

"I guess we should go this way," Violet said as she hesitantly took a few steps in that direction.

But the needle suddenly started to **spin** again. This time when it stopped, it was pointing to the **road on the left**. As soon as Violet changed course, the needle began to spin again.

"What if we split into two groups and each choose one direction," Colette suggested. "Then we can see what the needle does."

Pam laughed.

"Great idea!" she said.

But Will stopped them. "Better not, mouselets," he warned gently. "The imaginary worlds have their own **RULES**. Remember: Silvis said we would have to make a **decision**."

"So we should just choose a path RANDOMLY?" Violet asked, confused.

"Wait!" Paulina said suddenly. "I have another idea."

She pointed up at a flock of *seabirds* flying high in the sky.

They were heading **WEST**.

"I get it!" Nicky said. "Those birds must be flying toward water. If we head in the same direction, we're likely to find **LAPIS FALLS**!"

So the group took the road on the right. Soon the gravel under their paws turned the most amazing **shade** of coral.

"We did it!" Colette rejoiced.

In the distance, they could hear the **ROAR** of the Lapis Falls.

A CAGE OF WATER

The Thea Sisters and Will walked along the coral path all the way to the **FALLS**, which roared loudly, the water exploding in bright, **shiny** foam that looked like drops of pure crystal.

The mouselets stopped to admire the view.

But Will looked around anxiously. "I don't see the **Guardian Fairies** anywhere," he said, worried.

"You're right," Paulina replied. "And we don't have time to stop and wait."

"We'll have to ***keep going***," Colette said practically. "Maybe they will catch up with us along the way."

"Hey, look!" Nicky said, pointing to a

What a view!
How beautiful!

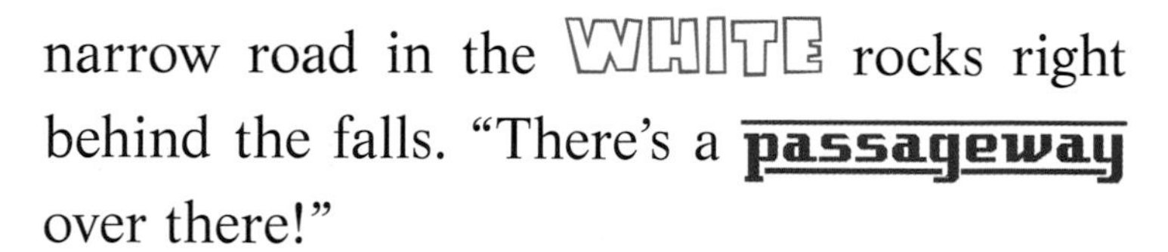

narrow road in the WHITE rocks right behind the falls. "There's a passageway over there!"

"Let's be careful," Will said cautiously. "That path looks very slippery."

As they walked along the path, the wall of falling water got CLOSER and CLOSER: It almost seemed like they were entering the heart of the falls. But there was still no sign of the Guardian Fairies.

"STOP!" a voice cried out suddenly. Two enormouse lobsters with pink shells and MENACING black eyes appeared on the path.

"WHAT ARE YOU DOING HERE?" one of the lobsters demanded.

"We were supposed to meet the Guardian Fairies," Paulina explained. "But when we didn't see them, we started walking toward the falls. WE DON'T HAVE TIME TO WASTE!"

But the lobsters seemed unmoved.

"**LET'S GET THEM!**" the other lobster cried as he hit his spear against a rock.

Suddenly, solid **WALLS OF WATER** rained down around Will and the mouselets on all **FOUR** sides.

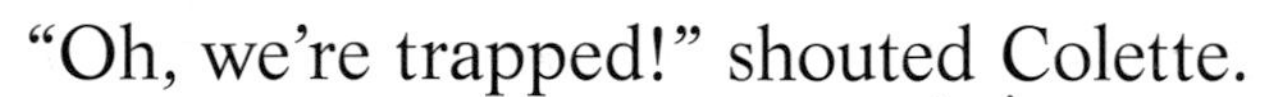

"Oh, we're trapped!" shouted Colette.

The water had formed a CAGE around them, blocking their movements in every direction.

As the Thea Sisters and Will tried to come up with a plan, they heard new voices around the water cage. Then two beautiful fairies in long blue gowns appeared.

"What is going on here?" one of the fairies asked.

"Venerable fairies, we have captured some intruders," explained the second lobster.

"Guardian Fairies, please, let us go!" Violet begged from inside the cage. "We have to speak to you! The CRYSTAL KINGDOM is in danger, and we're here to HELP!"

"Let them go," the second fairy ordered. "Let's hear what they have to say."

The first lobster hit his spear against the

rock again. The walls of water dried up as quickly as they had appeared.

Will and the Thea Sisters were free, and they were standing before the Guardian Fairies at last.

The fairies were very TALL and beautiful. Now that the Thea Sisters could look at them closely, they realized they were wearing golden tiaras atop their flowing blue hair.

Will bowed respectfully before them.

"Who are you, and why are you looking for us?" the fairies asked in unison.

"I am Will and these are the Thea Sisters," Will greeted them. "We are here in the CRYSTAL KINGDOM on a very important mission."

"We haven't heard of you before," the first fairy replied.

"How do we know you aren't lying,

travelers?" the second fairy added.

"The Crystal Fairies asked for our help defeating the dragon that is threatening the Crystal Kingdom," Colette explained.

"And we want to help wake Queen Tourmaline, too!" Nicky continued.

The fairies shook their heads, looking confused.

"Every morning we bathe in the falls because the water keeps us as pure as shiny crystals. At the same time, though, the water washes away our memories."

"Perhaps that's why you forgot that the kingdom is in danger!" Colette said.

"Yes, that is our sad fate," the first fairy replied.

"Therefore, if you want our help, you'll have to prove what you say is true," the second fairy said.

The Thea Sisters and Will exchanged a glance. What could they do? They had no choice.

Then Will pulled the light-emitting opal from his backpack and showed it to the Guardian Fairies.

"You have the opal!" The first fairy GASPED.

"Only the CRYSTAL FAIRIES could have given it to you!" the second fairy exclaimed.

The two Guardian Fairies exchanged a look.

"We believe you," they said in unison. "We will take you to the castle IMMEDIATELY."

"Thank you!" Will and the Thea Sisters replied.

The group of friends followed the fairies along the path, moving behind the waterfall. Soon they reached a dock where a mother-of-pearl boat seemed to be WAITING for them.

"We must sail on this **underground** river until we reach the Semi-Precious Stones Spring," the fairies explained. "The entrance to Joystone Castle is there."

With that, Will, the Thea Sisters, and the Guardian Fairies climbed aboard the sparkling boat.

A PRECIOUS SPRING

The trip on the underground river was very exciting. Colorful crystals and **precious stones** were visible from within the deep caves, while **shiny** fish followed the boat. Will and the Thea Sisters saw a brightly glowing circle in front of them.

"We have arrived," the fairies announced. "This is the Semi-Precious Stones Spring."

"Holey cheese!" Pam exclaimed in awe.

"The CRYSTALS in this spring are the purest in the whole kingdom," the fairies explained. "For this reason, the spring's water is extremely important to us."

Paulina put her paw in the water.

"It's crystal clear!" she exclaimed.

"Wow! It looks like a mirror," Colette marveled.

"The essence of all that is most precious in our kingdom is stored within these crystals," the fairies said.

"It would be **terrible** if the dragon ever found his way here," Violet said, a worried look on her snout.

"That won't happen," Will reassured her.

"You can get out here," the fairies said. "That staircase leads to the entrance to Joystone Castle."

"Are you coming with us?" Colette asked.

But the fairies shook their heads.

"We have to go back to **LAPIS FALLS**," they said. "That is where we belong: guarding the falls and the entrance to the Semi-Precious Stones Spring."

"**Thank you!**" the mouselets exclaimed.

"We should be thanking you," came the fairies' reply. Then they slowly sailed away on their mother-of-pearl boat.

Will and the Thea Sisters climbed the granite staircase and found themselves back on dry land again. In front of them was the entrance to Joystone Castle.

The crystal lock clicked and the gate began to open. An elegantly dressed fairy waited for them beyond the gate.

"Welcome," she greeted them. "My name is *Agatha*, and I am Queen Tourmaline's close friend and advisor."

JOYSTONE CASTLE

NORTH TOWER

WEST TOWER

GARDENS

CRYSTAL WALL

THRONE ROOM
PRIVATE QUARTERS
LIBRARY
EAST TOWER
SOUTH TOWER
ENTRANCE

"Nice to meet you!" Will replied. "My name is Will Mystery and these are the THEA SISTERS."

Agatha smiled.

"Please, come with me," she said.

The group of friends walked through the castle, taking in the castle's breathtaking decor.

Agatha led them to a large crystal door encrusted with **precious stones** of all sizes and colors.

"Here we are," she said. "These are **Queen Tourmaline's** private quarters."

Then she opened the door **slowly**.

Queen Tourmaline!
Come with me!

A TERRIBLE THREAT

When Will and the Thea Sisters entered the room, they saw Queen Tourmaline asleep on a **delicate** crystal bed, two fairies watching over her.

"These are the **guests** we were expecting," Agatha told the fairies. "This is Will Mystery and the Thea Sisters — Nicky, Violet, Paulina, Pamela, and Colette."

"Nice to meet you," replied the fairy in the **blue** dress. "I'm PEARL."

"And I'm *Galena*," added the second fairy, who was wearing a ***purple*** gown trimmed with sparkly silver ribbon. "We're so happy you are here."

"We got here as quickly as we could," Will

explained apologetically. "But it wasn't an easy journey. We even encountered the dragon who has caused so much **HARM** to your beautiful kingdom."

"Yes, the dragon," Pearl said, sighing. "We've been able to keep him away from the castle so far, but we haven't been able to stop him from destroying some of our kingdom's most **precious** stones!"

"And now the **Stone Desert** has spread all the way up to the Quartz Wall around our castle!" Galena added.

"Was that the **dark ring** we saw on the

magical living map in the Hall of the Seven Roses?" Violet asked Will.

"But of course!" Will exclaimed.

"This is the heart of the Crystal Kingdom," Paulina said thoughtfully. "So it makes sense that its protective wall is in DANGER, too."

"Dear fairies, please tell us what we can do to help," Colette said eagerly.

The fairies looked down at Tourmaline's bed, then asked the group of friends to come closer.

"Our queen has been like this for some time now," Pearl said softly.

"Wise ones from across the kingdom have come to see her, but no one understands how she fell into such a **deep sleep**, and no one has been able to wake her."

"What happened, exactly?" Nicky asked.

"We don't know," Agatha said sadly. "We

found Queen Tourmaline on the floor in the throne room, unconscious. Her **scepter** was on the floor, and the stone on its tip had shattered into a **THOUSAND PIECES**."

"What kind of stone was it?" Colette asked.

"It was a very special amber stone made from pure sunlight," Galena told them.

"This scepter belonged to the KING, Queen Tourmaline's father," Agatha explained.

"We found the queen's bracelet on the floor, too," Galena continued. "It was encrusted with precious stones from the **RUBY CAVES**."

"Was it shattered as well?"

Paulina asked, trying to gather as much evidence as possible.

"No, but all the rubies had turned to gray rocks," Galena replied.

"That must mean the dragon was here!" Paulina exclaimed. "Somehow, he was able to get into the castle without being detected."

"He must have gotten into the throne room, where he attacked the queen!" Violet added.

"Yes, that's what we think happened, too," Agatha said, sighing. "Though it's hard to believe no one saw him enter or leave."

"Whatever happened, the only thing to do now is STOP the dragon so Queen Tourmaline will awaken!" Pearl declared.

"You think the queen will wake up if we defeat the dragon?" Colette asked.

"We hope so!" Pearl replied anxiously.

"What do you suggest we do?" Will asked them.

"Only the wisest creature in the whole kingdom can answer that question," Galena replied.

"Her name is Amethyst and she lives at the top of LIGHT MOUNTAIN," Agatha explained.

"And you think she can tell us what happened to your queen?" Nicky asked.

"Yes," Pearl replied. "Amethyst owns a very special crystal, the Query Quartz."

"She is the only one who is able to interpret the stone's answers," Agatha continued.

"But why haven't you gone to

see her yourselves?" Will asked them, confused.

We aren't allowed to leave **Joystone Castle**," Galena explained. "Like all the other fairies in the Crystal Kingdom, we cannot

go TOO FAR from the place we **guard**."

"If you can give us **directions** to Light Mountain, we will help you," Will said.

"Wait here," Agatha told them. She left the room and returned with a **rolled-up** scroll. "This is an old map of the Crystal Kingdom," Agatha explained. "It will help you find the mountain."

She unrolled the **YELLOW** scroll and pointed to a spot on the map.

DESERT OF ROCKS
AND DUST

ETERNAL WOODS

STONE
CIRCLES

NIGHT GEMS
PATH

JOYSTONE
CASTLE

QUARTZ
WALL

DARK CAVES

CITRINE RIVER

RUBY
CAVES

JADE
JUNGLE

BLUE ONYX
VALLEY

CIRCLE OF INTEN
LIGHT

CRYSTAL WOODS

SAPPHIRE SEA

ISLAND ENTRANCE

STONE OF THE DEEP

WAVY PATH

EMERALD FOREST

ROCKY CRYSTAL PATH

UNDERGROUD RIVER TO THE SEMI-PRECIOUS STONES SPRING

LAPIS FALLS

BLUE TOPAZ

LIGHT MOUNTAIN

Crystal Kingdom

"Here is LIGHT MOUNTAIN," she said. "You can see the top CLEARLY from the foot of the mountain."

"You'll have to cross the magical waters of the Citrine River to get there," Pearl added.

"Be CAREFUL!" Agatha warned. "The only way to cross the river is by stepping on the Citrine Quartz Crystals, one step at a time, in exactly the right order."

"And how do we know the RIGHT order?" Paulina wondered.

"The correct order is determined by the quartz," Agatha replied cryptically.

"Well, let's get going," Will said. "There's no time to waste!"

Will and the Thea Sisters looked at the sleeping queen one more time before they turned to go. Then they paused at the

entrance to the castle for one more moment while they waved good-bye to the fairies.

"Thank you for your help!" Agatha, Pearl, and Galena called as their friends walked past the Quartz Wall. The **MISSION** was on!

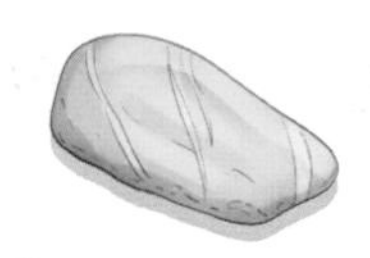

A DIFFICULT PATH

As Will and the Thea Sisters walked along the path to LIGHT MOUNTAIN, they admired the unique *crystal flowers* that lined the way.

Suddenly, a flower caught Colette's eye, and she bent down for a closer LOOK.

"OH NO!" she exclaimed. "This must have been a **beautiful** crystal flower once, but now it's just **GRAY** rock."

"Mouselets, we absolutely must stop the dragon before it's **too late**!" Pam said.

The friends continued their journey, stopping along the way for brief rests to keep

their energy up. Finally, Paulina checked the map the fairies had given them.

"We should be close now," she said.

"Hmmm," Will said as he studied the map. "The river should be ahead, but why can't we see it?"

Nicky and Pam took a few more steps, and then suddenly stopped.

"There it is!" they cried in unison.

The others caught up with them and discovered a small cliff just ahead. Below it, the Citrine River flowed through a BIG VALLEY.

"How are we going to get down there?" Violet asked. "This CLIFF is very steep."

"And we don't have the right gear to climb DOWN," Nicky added.

"Violet and Nicky are right," Will agreed. "We'll have to find a different way."

"Wait!" Paulina exclaimed suddenly. She

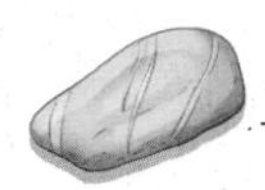

pointed at a grove of trees. "Look over there. Are those stairs behind the trees?"

Violet got closer.

"You're right, Paulina!" she said excitedly. "It looks like they were CARVED into the rock. They go all the way down to the river!"

"They look like they've been here for ages, but they seem STURDY," Paulina remarked as she peered at the stone closely.

"In any case, we should be **wary**," Will said cautiously. "They are very narrow. Be careful where you place your paws. You don't want to slip and FALL!"

The group of friends slowly climbed down, step by step, until they reached the valley and the river below.

The *Citrine River* was flowing by right in front of them, through golden quartz rocks.

"Now all we have to do is get ACROSS," Will said. He was about to step on a stone when Nicky cried out.

"Stop!" she squeaked. "Remember what the fairies said? It could be DANGEROUS! I'm pretty good at crossing rivers — let me go FIRST."

"Okay," Will agreed.

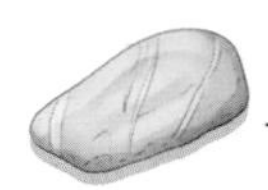

"Lead the way and we'll FOLLOW."

Nicky walked to the shore to study the route. Then she carefully stepped on a quartz rock. It immediately sank into the river, causing her to lose her footing.

"I'm fine," Nicky reassured her friends as she regained her balance. "But I'm trying to understand something."

"Me, too," Paulina chimed in. "The fairies said to step on the rocks in the right order, and that the quartz would determine the order. But what does that mean?"

"It must mean that some rocks are stable while others will sink into the water if we step on them," Nicky mused thoughtfully.

Then the mouselet returned to her friends and climbed back UP a few stone steps. From there, she could look DOWN on the quartz rocks.

"What are you doing?" Colette asked.

"I want to study the exact location of each QUARTZ in the river," she explained.

"**Mouselets, I've got it!**" Nicky exclaimed happily, drawing a sketch in the notebook she carried in her pocket.

"We have to take the fairies' instructions literally and look at the exact shape of the Crystal Quartz!" The Thea Sisters looked at her, confused.

Nicky showed her friends the SKETCH she had drawn in her notebook and explained what she meant.

"See?" she asked, pointing. "Some rocks are laid out in a shape similar to the quartz ones. I am sure that if we STEP on these rocks only, we should be able to reach the other side **safely**!"

"Well, it's worth a try," Paulina said.

Nicky was the first to make it all the way across the river, which proved her hypothesis. Will and the Thea Sisters followed closely behind her and were on the other bank with

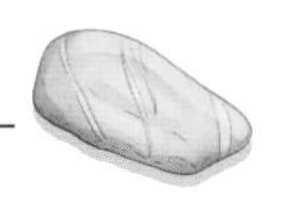

Nicky in no time. Then they all continued to walk together on their journey toward LIGHT MOUNTAIN.

THE FOOT OF THE MOUNTAIN

Will and the Thea Sisters continued quietly, exhausted from their long journey so far.

Then Will noticed a **BRIGHT LIGHT** directly ahead.

"Look!" he exclaimed, pointing.

The grove of trees in front of them thinned out and was replaced by a hill encrusted with precious crystal gemstones.

"Holey cheese, what an **amazing** sight!" Pam cried in awe.

"I don't think the dragon has been here yet," Violet remarked. "These stones are shining too brightly."

"Let's hope he NEVER gets here!" Colette continued, admiring the view.

Then she and her friends began climbing the GRANITE stairs that wrapped around the mountain, seeming to go on forever.

"Phew!" Pamela said as she climbed.

"These steps seem like they'll NEVER end."

"Come on, mouselets!" Will said encouragingly from the front of the group. "I think we're almost at the TOP!"

Sure enough, a few minutes later, the group of friends reached the sparkling SUMMIT.

"That must be Amethyst's house," Violet said, pointing to a small cottage decorated with many purple crystals.

Paulina walked up to the door and knocked gently.

"Come in!" a sweet voice replied.

The mouselets and Will entered the house. Inside, a fairy was busy decorating an enormouse tapestry.

"Welcome to Light Mountain, friends," she greeted them warmly, looking up from her work with kind eyes. "What brings you all this way?"

"We're very sorry to interrupt your work, **Amethyst**, but we need your **help**," Will explained.

"I suppose the Joystone fairies sent you here," Amethyst said.

"Yes, that's right," Nicky replied. "They are **worried** about the Crystal Kingdom and Queen Tourmaline."

"We're here because you're the only one who can **help us**," Violet added.

"Very well," Amethyst replied. Then she stood and walked to a small round table in the corner of the cottage. There was a **GIGANTIC** quartz in the center of the table.

"This is the **Query Quartz**," Amethyst explained. "As you place your right paw on its surface, each one of you may ask a question. The quartz will change **COLOR**

and shade depending on its answers, which I will interpret for you."

Will and the Thea Sisters talked for a few minutes, then each put their paws on the quartz, as the fairy had asked them to.

"**We're ready!**" Will said at last. They asked their questions one by one.

After a few moments, the quartz changed into the many colors of the **rainbow**. It

was so beautiful Will and the mouselets were squeakless.

Amethyst studied the answers while walking around the group of friends, drawing *SKETCHES* in her notebook. Then, finally, she sat down again.

"The quartz has answered some of your **questions**," she said. "As for the others, well, there are some things the quartz simply

1. A dragon called Goldfire is roaming the kingdom. His body is covered in golden armor. He is under a spell cast by an evil wizard.

2. Goldfire is looking for a specific precious stone, and he won't stop until he finds it.

3. Queen Tourmaline is under a spell cast by the same wizard who imprisoned Goldfire. Only the Sweet Awakening Gem can break the spell.

4. Before you can awaken the queen, you must stop the dragon.

5. If you want to protect the kingdom, find the Ancient Amber Tree, which is the source of the amber forged from pure sunlight.

6. The tree is the only guardian of the secret of the amber.

does not know. Now listen closely to its **replies**."

After she had read her notes aloud, Amethyst put down her pen and notebook.

"This is all the quartz can tell you," she explained. "I'm afraid it cannot reveal anything else."

"Your help has been invaluable," Will replied gratefully.

But Paulina was worried.

"How will we find this Ancient Amber Tree?" she asked, concerned. "We've already asked the quartz all we can."

"I can tell you where to find the tree!" Amethyst said.

"Oh, thank you!" Nicky exclaimed.

"The Crystal Fairies gave us this map," Will said, pulling it out of his backpack. "Can you **SHOW** us the way to the tree?"

"The tree is here, in the Eternal Woods," she said, pointing. "It's a very thick and mysterious forest, guarded by the brave and proud Golden Elves.

"They will welcome you kindly, but beware: They are fierce guardians of their forest, and they can be suspicious of unexpected visitors."

"We will be careful," Will reassured her. "And now we'd better go."

"Climb down the stairs you took to get here," Amethyst said. "Once you reach the bottom, turn right and cross the river. You'll soon see a LARGE GATE."

Then she took something out of a drawer and gave it to Will.

"This is the key to unlock it," Amethyst explained. "Once you're through the gate, the Night Gems Path begins. It's a

SECRET passageway that only the elves and I know about."

"Thank you again for your help," Will replied.

"Yes, thank you!" the Thea Sisters echoed gratefully.

Then the group continued on their important quest.

THE ETERNAL WOODS

Will and the Thea Sisters climbed down the stairs and followed the fairy's directions until they arrived at the entrance to the Night Gems Path.

Will put the key in the lock and turned it. Suddenly, the gate lit up with a BRIGHT LIGHT and opened. The friends took a few steps into the tunnel.

"Holey cheese!" Pam exclaimed. "We're about to enter an underground garden!"

"Look, the walls are completely covered in flowers!" Nicky remarked.

"How lovely," Colette said, sighing as the gate closed behind them.

"This kingdom grows more beautiful —

and more mysterious — with every turn," Violet murmured.

"And we'll do everything in our power to protect it," Will declared confidently.

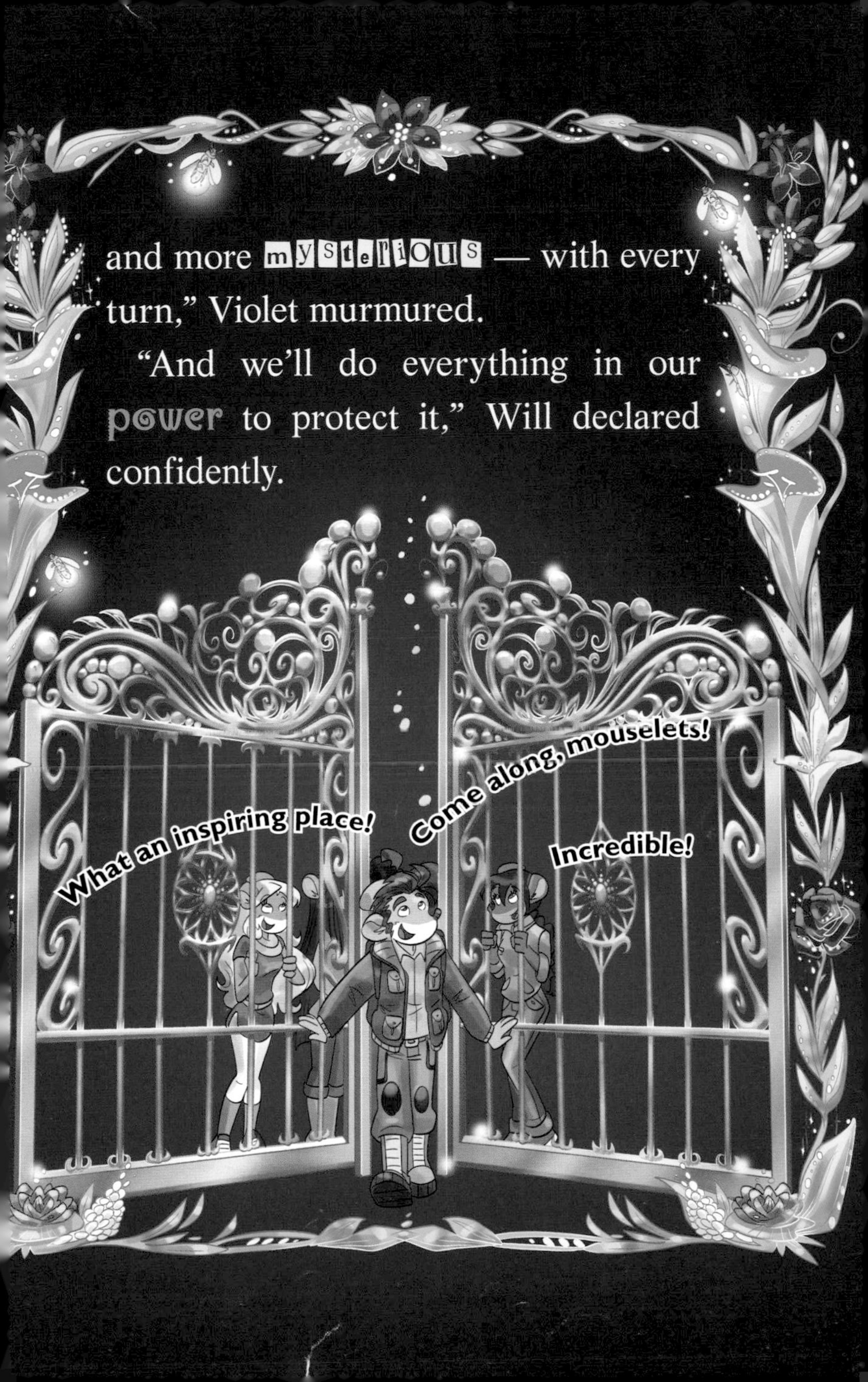

When they reached the end of the tunnel, they were enveloped by the earthy **smell** of pine needles and tree bark.

"Wow!" Nicky remarked, taking a deep breath. "Now I understand why the Golden Elves are so fond of these woods."

"Speaking of the elves, I **wonder** where they are," Paulina said.

Before anyone could reply, Colette let out a squeak.

"Yikes!" Colette cried out. "Who was that? Someone touched my fur!"

Then Pamela squeaked suddenly.

"ME, TOO!" she exclaimed. "I felt something around my paw!"

"What's going on?!" Violet exclaimed, scared.

"**It's the trees . . . look!**" Paulina squeaked, pointing to a branch that was stretching out toward them.

"Quick!" Will shouted. "RUN!"

But the branches seemed to grow longer as they reached out, grabbing at Will and the Thea Sisters. The mouselets quickly realized there was no way they could OUTRUN the trees.

Instead, Will began talking to them.

"Please stop!" he said. "We're not the enemies! We were sent here by the Crystal Fairies, and we're looking for the noble Golden Elves."

Unfortunately, the trees just tightened their grip.

"Help!" the mouselets cried.

"What are we going to do?" Violet asked.

Then, suddenly, they heard the sweet sound of a flute in the distance.

The trees loosened their grip IMMEDIATELY. Then an elf stepped out from behind a tree.

"Hello," the elf said. "Who are you, and why are you here in our woods?"

His voice was as sweet as the sound emanating from his flute.

Hello . . .
who are you?

Will explained the reason for the group's **visit**. The elf smiled in reply, and beckoned for Will and the Thea Sisters to FOLLOW him deeper into the Eternal Woods.

THE SECRET OF THE AMBER

Eventually, the elf stopped walking.

"Here we are," he said simply. "This is our VILLAGE."

He pointed to a bunch of small homes built into LARGE tree trunks.

"Please wait for me here," he told them.

Then he walked into one of the houses and came out shortly after. He was followed by another elf who was wearing a long golden cape and a crown.

"Greetings, visitors," the elf said. "My name is Arbor, Lord of the Golden Elves. Varno just explained that you were sent by the Crystal Fairies, and that you would like me to take you to the Ancient

Amber Tree."

"That's right," Colette replied. "Unfortunately, the Crystal Kingdom is in great danger. A dragon named GOLDFIRE has been looking for something — and destroying all that is good in his quest."

"We don't know what he's looking for," Paulina added. "But we have to STOP him as soon as possible!"

"I am sorry your journey here was so difficult," the Lord of the Elves replied. "Much as I would like to, I CANNOT fulfill your request."

"WHY NOT?" Pam asked, incredulous.

"The Ancient Amber Tree is extremely fragile, and it is my duty to protect it," he explained.

"But the kingdom's safety is at stake here," Paulina responded.

"And Queen Tourmaline is in grave danger, too!" Violet added.

"What did you say?" Arbor asked. "The queen is in DANGER?"

Violet explained what had happened. With every word the elf grew more worried.

Finally, after a few moments of silence, Arbor spoke.

"Your purpose is honorable and your **hearts** are pure," he said solemnly. "I will take you to the **tree**."

Then Varno, another elf, and Arbor led Will and the mouselets out of the village and down a **dirt** path.

At last they reached an enormouse tree with a thick, **REDDISH-BROWN** trunk.

"This is the oldest tree in the Eternal Woods: the **Ancient Amber Tree**," Arbor explained. "All the elves respect this tree because the **wisdom of the woods** resides within its bark."

He stepped closer to the tree and very **gently** placed his hand on its trunk.

A moment later, he removed his hand, and with it, a thin **SHEET OF PAPER**.

"Wow!" Violet gasped.

"Amazing," Paulina murmured.

"Here is the tree's answer to your question," Arbor said.

"What language is it written in?" Pamela asked. She tried peering over the elf's shoulder to take a look, but she didn't recognize the MARKS on the page.

"The tree speaks the ancient language of the Golden Elves," Arbor replied.

"Will you please read it to us?" Colette asked, intrigued.

"According to the tree, there are two unique pieces of amber in the Crystal Kingdom: the Sunlight Amber and the Star Amber," Arbor read. "A wizard imprisoned a fairy named Esmeralda inside the Star Amber."

"What does that have to do with the dragon?" Paulina asked, confused.

Arbor held up his hand gently.

"Wait," he said. "There's more to the

story. Esmeralda's beloved was one of the Knights of Crystal Rock. He served Queen Tourmaline's father, Eliodoro, as Hand of the King. But when the wizard cursed Esmeralda, he cursed the knight, too! First he turned the knight into a dragon named Goldfire. Then the wizard imprisoned the dragon inside the Sunlight Amber!"

"So the dragon escaped and is looking for his beloved fairy in all the crystals?" Pamela asked.

"The poor knight!" Colette said. "So the dragon's only been behaving badly because of this wizard's EVIL spell!"

"The kingdom will be **peaceful** again only if we find the dragon and help him undo the spell," Arbor concluded.

"At last we know what GOLDFIRE is looking for," Nicky said.

"Right, but where is he?" Paulina chimed in.

"Perhaps we can answer that question," Varno said.

Everyone looked at him, intrigued.

"The dragon was last seen a short time ago," the elf continued. "He was on the way to the Desert of Rocks and Dust."

Arbor didn't look surprised.

"He must think his beloved is there somewhere," he said.

"Why do you think so?" Colette asked.

"No one would dare enter the Desert of Rocks and Dust unless he had a very good reason to do so," Varno explained. "It's a desolate place full of **horrible**, dangerous creatures."

"Is it far from here?" Will asked.

"It's located on the outskirts of the Crystal

Kingdom, but I know a CONNECTING path from the Eternal Woods," came Varno's reply.

"From what you say, it sounds difficult," Paulina remarked.

"Not if you have help," Arbor replied, whistling LOUDLY.

Suddenly, six huge golden hawks flew in and landed next to the group.

"What extraordinary creatures!" Nicky gasped, admiring the giant birds.

"These birds will fly you to the desert," Arbor said. Then the Lord of the Elves grabbed a GOLDEN DAGGER from his belt and handed it to the Thea Sisters.

"Take this," he said. "It's the most POWERFUL

weapon in the entire kingdom. It can slice through any substance. But remember: Only someone with a **pure** and **brave** heart will be able to use it."

"Thank you, Arbor," Will replied. "I promise we will use it wisely."

"Go now," Arbor replied. "I wish you much success on your important **MISSION**!"

"Thank you!" Will and the Thea Sisters replied as they climbed onto the hawks and flew off on the next leg of their journey.

A VORTEX OF SAND

Flying on the golden hawks was an unforgettable experience. They held on tight to the GOLDEN FEATHERS. The birds soared over the steep rock walls of the **NARROW ROCKY CANYON** that connected the Eternal Woods to the Desert of Rocks and Dust.

"We must be getting closer by now," Nicky said.

"You're right," Will replied as he scanned the **horizon**. "We've been flying for a while now, so we can't be too far."

Then the landscape suddenly changed from **COLORFUL** crystals to dry, dusty **sand**.

They had arrived in the **Desert of Rocks and Dust**.

The hawks began their descent, landing **gently**.

"Thank you for your help, **friends**!" Will exclaimed. The hawks lowered their beaks to say good-bye and then **flapped their wings** and took off, leaving the group of friends behind in the middle of the sand.

Thanks for your help!

The mouselets and Will were trying to get their bearings when an **enormouse** red **cloud** appeared on the horizon.

It looked like a tornado and seemed to be **swallowing** up anything in its path.

"**LET'S GET OUT OF HERE!**" Paulina shouted. She grabbed Violet's paw and the two mice began to *run*.

The others followed quickly on their paws, but no matter how fast they ran, the **vortex of sand** was even faster.

"It's almost here!" Colette screamed.

Moments later, the group of friends was engulfed by the **tornado**. Will, Pam, Colette, Violet, Nicky, and Paulina were yanked up by the unstoppable strength of the **dusty wind**.

"Paulina, grab my paw!" Nicky shouted, bracing herself.

"Colette, can you **grab** mine?" Pam cried.

The Thea Sisters held one another's paws tightly, trying to stand up to the ***wind***.

"Will!" Paulina called out. "Where are you?"

"HERE!" he replied, tightly grabbing the paw she extended to him.

Now that they were all together again, the reddish sandstorm was a little **less frightening**.

"What do we do **now**?" Pamela asked.

But she couldn't hear anyone's reply over the **shrieking** sound of the whirlwind.

"I'm so tired," Violet complained. "My arms hurt!"

"Don't give up, Vi!" Colette replied immediately, shouting to be heard over the ***wind***.

"Hold on **TIGHT** and don't let go!" Paulina added.

"**WAIT!**" Nicky exclaimed suddenly. "**THE STORM IS SLOWING!**"

Little by little, the air CLEARED and the sand stopped blowing. In a few minutes, the **vortex** had disappeared. Will and the

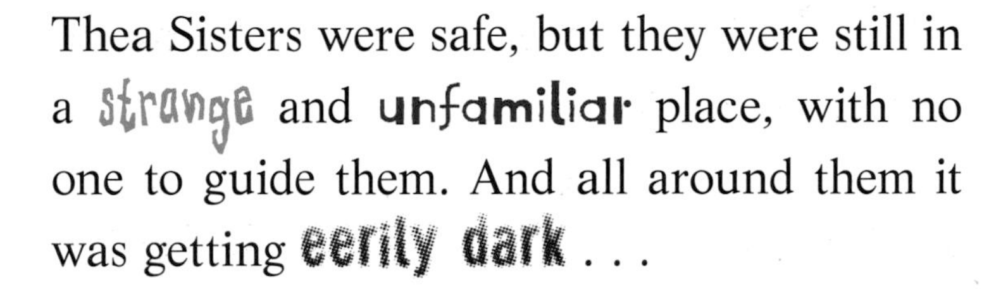

Thea Sisters were safe, but they were still in a strange and unfamiliar place, with no one to guide them. And all around them it was getting eerily dark . . .

AN ENORMOUSE SURPRISE!

"I've never experienced anything like that in my life!" Pam remarked, shaking sand off her fur.

"We're lucky we weren't HURT and that it moved away quickly," Nicky added.

But when she tried to get up, she realized she couldn't move: Her paws had sunk in the ground up to her ankles.

"Mouselets, don't move!" Will warned.

"Oh no!" Colette exclaimed, looking down. "Don't tell me we're standing in quicksand?!"

"They look more like small OBSIDIAN STONES than sand," Paulina said, studying the ground closely. The tiny round rocks looked like marbles. Pam tried to take a step

but immediately realized that wasn't a **good idea**.

"We can't move, otherwise we'll sink **deeper**," Nicky said.

"What should we do, then?" Violet asked.

"I have an idea, but one of you has to help me," Will replied.

"I'll help," Paulina said. "What do you need me to do?"

"Open my backpack and take out the rope," he said. "But please move slowly."

Paulina took a deep **breath** to help her focus. Then, moving slowly and gently, she reached out toward Will. Delicately, she opened the backpack and reached in with her paw. She felt a lot of tools and objects. Finally, she felt the rope.

"I've got it!" she cried. She pulled it out and slowly handed it to Will. The Thea

Sisters looked on, squeakless.

"I'm going to try to lasso those **BOULDERS** over there," Will explained as he knotted a large loop in the rope. "Then we can pull ourselves out of this obsidian quicksand and get to **safety**!"

Will took a deep breath and tossed the rope. **HE MISSED!**

"Try again, Will!" Nicky said encouragingly. "Maybe aim a little HIGHER."

Will tossed the rope again, and this time is **WORKED**! The lasso landed around a large, **STURDY** boulder.

"**Great job!**" the Thea Sisters rejoiced

"Now, everyone, grab on to the rope," Will instructed. "If we want to have any hope of getting out of here, we'll have to **work together**! We can do this!"

The Thea Sisters held the rope and pulled with all their strength.

Will, Paulina, and Violet were the first ones to get out of the **obsidian quicksand**. Then they quickly helped their friends.

"We made it!" Colette rejoiced.

"Thank you, Will!" Nicky exclaimed. "And thank you, Paulina! You two saved us with your quick thinking."

Will began to retract the rope, but suddenly he felt a YANK from the other end.

"Huh?!" Will gasped, perplexed.

Just then, he and the Thea Sisters realized that the gray mass wasn't actually a **BOULDER**. Instead, they had lassoed a

GIGANTIC STONE TROLL!

THE STONE CIRCLES

Will and the Thea Sisters looked at one another, suddenly afraid.

But before they had the chance to squeak one word, **two trolls** popped up right behind the first one!

"***What should we do?***" Pam whispered.

"We can't go back," Paulina replied softly. "The obsidian quicksand is that way . . ."

"We're trapped!" Colette exclaimed.

Will decided the best thing to do was CONFRONT the trolls. He boldly took a step forward.

"Hello!" he said. "I'm sorry for lassoing you. We mean no harm. My name is Will Mystery, and I am on a mission with these

mouselets to help save the Crystal Kingdom from **DANGER**!"

At first, the trolls didn't move or respond. They stood there, **frozen** like statues! Then the **LARGEST** troll spoke.

"You cannot cross this land without our permission!" he said in a **deep**, booming voice. "As of now, you are our **PRISONERS**!"

Then he turned to the other trolls and gave them an order: "GET THEM!"

Before Will and the mouselets could react, the trolls grabbed them and carried them off to a cave deep underground.

"What is this place?" Pam had the courage to ask.

"Welcome to the STONE CIRCLES, the scariest prison in the entire kingdom," the second troll said, bursting out in deep laughter that ECHOED off the rock walls.

"WHO ARE THEY?" asked a troll who was standing guard in front of what looked like a prison cell.

"Brand-new prisoners," the first troll said with a grin. "Aren't you happy?"

"Yes, what an excellent gift!" the guard replied with a cackle.

"Now we're going back out on patrol," the

first troll told him. "Make sure they don't **escape**!"

"Don't worry." The guard chuckled. "No one can **escape** from my prison!"

Then he opened one of the cells and **pushed** Will and the mouselets inside.

"I hope you like it, because you'll be here for a **WHILE**," he said. Then he burst out laughing again.

The Thea Sisters and Will looked around in dismay: They were trapped in a **DARK CELL**, locked by a heavy gate.

"I think we are in serious trouble," Colette whispered.

"Don't worry," Will encouraged them. "We'll find a way out somehow."

"We'll have to figure it out quickly," Paulina added. "Otherwise GOLDFIRE will destroy more of the kingdom."

"Are you talking about a golden dragon?" came a soft voice from the DARKEST corner of the cell.

"Who's there?" Will asked.

"My name is Piro," the creature replied as he stepped out of the DARK. "I'm a leprechaun from Sweet Garnet Valley."

"Are you a prisoner, too?" Will asked.

Piro nodded in reply.

"Have you ever tried to *escape*?" Pam asked.

"Yes!" Piro replied. "But it's impossible. The walls are dug out of the hardest rock, and there is only one exit, GUARDED by the trolls. I gave up. At least I have someone to talk to, now that you're here."

"We need to get out of here as soon as possible," Will replied. "If you want to, you can come with us."

"You just mentioned a dragon," Paulina pointed out. "Have you heard about him?"

"Yes, some of my friends were talking about him before the **TROLLS** captured me," Piro replied.

"What did they say?" Colette asked.

"If I remember correctly, they were saying that a big dragon with golden armor had been captured by the **Dark Fairies**."

"Who are the **Dark Fairies**?" Paulina asked.

"They are mysterious creatures," Piro explained. "No one knows for sure, but rumor has it that once upon a time, they were quite beautiful. They lived in the **desert** and eventually they became **JEALOUS** of the Crystal Fairies. Their envy turned them into dark, mysterious creatures."

"Where can we find them?" Violet asked.

"They live in the gloomy Dark Caves," the leprechaun went on. "But I wouldn't go there if I were you."

"Well, we can't go anywhere until we **BREAK OUT** of this prison!" Will reminded him. Then he explained to Piro who they were and the reason for their **MISSION**.

"If the trolls were to find out a big **golden dragon** is being held prisoner by the Dark Fairies, they would probably want to snatch him from them, right?" Paulina asked.

Piro looked thoughtful. "Trolls are not interested in **gold** nor in **CRYSTALS**," he replied. "But the Dark Fairies are their **archenemies** for sure!"

"Then we must convince the trolls to **free** the dragon and **enrage** the fairies," Colette suggested.

"**Good idea!**" Will exclaimed.

"The best thing to do is to **OUTSMART** the trolls," the leprechaun said. Then he walked to the front of the cell and called out to the guard.

"Hey, troll!" Piro cried.

"What do you want?" the troll yelled, walking over.

"I have some information to share with you . . ." Piro said temptingly.

"Oh yeah?" the guard replied. "Well, I'm not interested."

"Really?" Piro went on. "It's about the Dark Fairies . . ."

"What about them?" the troll replied.

"I heard they CAPTURED a prisoner that they have been chasing for a long time," the leprechaun whispered.

"Go on." The guard was definitely interested now.

"It's a golden dragon," Piro went on. "It would be a great insult to them if someone were to free him, don't you think?"

The troll seemed to think it over before he turned and walked away.

"Now we wait and see," Piro replied.

After a few minutes, a group of **trolls** came back to open the cell gate.

"We're taking you all to the Dark Caves to see if you're telling the truth about the dragon," the troll leader told the leprechaun.

The trolls listened to the plan. They lined up the prisoners and led them out of the Stone Circles. Then they proceeded to walk to the **DARK CAVES**.

THE MYSTERIOUS DARK FAIRIES

"Here we are," the leader of the trolls announced as they approached the caves. "This is the entrance."

"Well, now you'll have to leave," the leprechaun told the trolls.

"Piro is right!" Colette chimed in. "If the fairies see you, it would ruin our plan."

"Let us take care of it since we're smaller and quieter," Paulina added.

The trolls considered this.

"We agree," the leader announced. "But how will we know when the dragon is FREE?"

"That's easy," Piro said, smiling. "You'll hear the ANGRY SCREAMS of the Dark Fairies!"

The trolls burst out **LAUGHING**. Then they let their prisoners continue on their own.

"Well, we managed to get away from the trolls — for now," Pam remarked.

"Yes, but the difficult part is yet to come," Will replied.

Together, the group cautiously approached the entrance to the caves.

The mouselets were about to follow Will into the cave when the leprechaun stopped them.

"Before you go, I must say GOOD-BYE," Piro said.

"You're not coming with us?" Violet asked, confused.

"I'm afraid I can't," he replied. "Like all creatures in the Crystal Kingdom, I can't travel too far from my home. The Dark Caves are too far from my village, which is beyond the mountains."

"We understand," Violet said.

"Thank you for helping us," Nicky added. "If it wasn't for you, we would still be the trolls' prisoners!"

"Good luck on your mission to protect the

Crystal Kingdom," Piro said. "We are friends forever now!"

Will and the Thea Sisters waved good-bye to the leprechaun and then stepped into the CAVE.

"Let's be very quiet," Will warned them. "The fairies won't like unexpected visitors."

Cautiously, the friends walked deep into the DARK CAVES. Suddenly, they heard a rhythmic sound ECHOING through the caves.

"I hear footsteps," Colette whispered. "Quick! Let's hide in that tunnel!"

They dashed into a tiny passageway and peeked out to see three beautiful creatures with long, shiny hair and pearly-white skin glide by. A small FLINT BLADE hung from each of their belts.

Will and the Thea Sisters held their breath

until the fairies had passed. Then they stepped out of their hiding place and continued on their way.

"We're lucky they didn't see us," Will said, breathing a sigh of relief. "We have to be more careful. Now that I've seen them, I'm more convinced that it won't be easy to confront these Dark Fairies."

"Look!" Violet pointed. "There's something

glowing over there!"

Farther inside the cave, they could see a faint GLIMMER of light down one of the tunnels.

Will and the Thea Sisters cautiously headed down the tunnel. Finally, they reached the glowing light.

"It's him!" Colette gasped. "It's Goldfire!"

The gigantic golden dragon was tied

up with ropes in the middle of the underground cavern.

"Holey cheese, he's even bigger than I remembered!" Pam exclaimed.

"He looked so much **smaller** when we saw him in the Emerald Forest!" Nicky said.

"Remember what Silvis told us?" Will asked. "He must have grown larger as he turned **PRECIOUS CRYSTALS** throughout the kingdom into rocks."

"Those must be incredibly strong ropes," Pam remarked.

"We have to figure out a way to free him," Colette said.

At that moment, the dragon spoke. "Who's there?" he huffed, his voice **LOW** and **deep**.

Colette slowly leaned in toward the creature and whispered to him.

"Please be quiet, GOLDFIRE," she said. "If

we make too much noise, the fairies will hear us."

"Who are you?" the dragon replied. "And how do you know my name?"

"My name is Colette, and my friends and I are here to **help you**."

"I don't need your help!" came the dragon's **angry** reply.

"Shhh!" Colette shushed him. "We know the truth. We know you're looking for the **Star Amber** so you can free your beloved Esmeralda."

"You know about Esmeralda?" Goldfire asked, incredulous.

"We know you and Esmeralda were the victims of an **EVIL SPELL**," Colette said, waving her friends closer.

"That **EVIL WIZARD**!" Goldfire scoffed. "Esmeralda and I were so happy until he came along! He cast that spell just to get even with King Eliodoro!"

"He was Queen Tourmaline's father, correct?" Will asked.

"Yes, that's right," the dragon replied. "I was the bravest knight in his service, and I helped fight the wizard. But because of this, **my beloved** and I were cast under his spell."

The Thea Sisters and Will looked at one another. They had no idea how they would free the dragon, but they knew they had to come up with a plan quickly or they would be in **GREAT DANGER**.

A DIFFICULT TASK

The mouselets and Will tried to loosen the ropes, but they were as thick as steel cables.

"Holey cheese, these are HEAVY!" Pam exclaimed.

"They aren't ropes," the dragon explained. "They are IRON CABLES. The fairies forged them out of a SPECIAL steel they created in their metalworking workshop."

"How strong are they?" Colette asked

"I tried MELTING them with my fiery breath, cutting them with my claws, and shearing them with my jaws, but nothing worked," Goldfire said.

"We'll have to come up with another plan," Will said, thinking it over.

Suddenly, Will's snout lit up.

"Of course!" he exclaimed. He quickly rummaged through his backpack and pulled out the dagger Arbor had given him.

"**The Dagger of the Golden Elves!**" Paulina said excitedly. "Arbor said it could cut through anything!"

At that moment, they heard steps coming from the one of the dark caves.

"It's the **Dark Fairies**," the dragon told them, frightened.

"What should we do?" Violet asked, worried.

"Quick, hide!" Goldfire replied. "If the Dark Fairies **capture** you, we'll never get out of here!"

Will and the mouselets

scrambled to find a hiding place.

"OVER THERE!" Will said, pointing to a recess in the back of the cave.

"It's a dead end," Violet argued, shaking her snout. "We'll be trapped."

"We should split up," Colette suggested. "Some of us can distract the fairies while the others stay and free the dragon."

"It's a RISKY plan," Will objected.

"There's no time and we really don't have a choice," Paulina said quickly. "I think it will work!"

The other Thea Sisters agreed.

"Once I'm free, I can help get us out of here," the dragon promised. "You have my word."

In the meantime, the footsteps grew closer and closer.

"I'll be the bait," Colette said.

"We'll go with you," Pam and Nicky said.

"Fine, then we'll stay here to free Goldfire," Will agreed reluctantly, looking at Paulina and Violet. "Please be very **careful**!"

Quietly, they all got ready for action.

Will, Paulina, and Violet **hid** under the dragon's wing, while Colette, Pam, and Nicky got ready to deal with the fairies.

"Who are you?" the Dark Fairies asked as soon as they saw the three mouselets. "**STOP!**"

Colette, Pam, and Nicky didn't reply. Instead, they ran as fast as their tails could go. They dashed down one of the **tunnels**, trying to lure the fairies as far away as possible from the cave where Goldfire was imprisoned.

The fairies ***took off*** after them, leaving

the dragon — and the mice hiding undetected under his wings — behind. Their plan was working so far!

THE POWER OF A PURE HEART

While the fairies chased Colette, Pam, and Nicky, Will began CUTTING the first cable.

"It's really strong," he remarked. "I've never seen anything like this."

"Don't give up, Will," Paulina said. "You can do it!"

Will knew he had TOO LITTLE time and too many cables to cut through. He realized if he kept going as he was, he would **NEVER** be able to free the dragon.

"This has to work," Violet said. "Arbor can't be wrong."

"He said his **dagger** would help us!" Paulina agreed.

"Perhaps I'm using it in the wrong way," Will said thoughtfully.

Then he remembered the elf's words: *Only a pure and brave heart will be able to use it.*

He had an idea. What if he closed his eyes and focused hard on the **wonders** of the Crystal Kingdom and his resolve to help **Queen Tourmaline** and her subjects. When he started cutting again, the dagger released a **BRIGHT, POWERFUL BLUE LIGHT** and the first cable snapped easily. A moment later, the second, third, and fourth cables snapped as **easily** as if they were **FINE** strands of hair.

"I knew you could do it!" Paulina smiled at Will.

Will had **CUT** through all but **THREE** of the cables, when the trio heard the sound of the Dark Fairies' footsteps again.

Will, Violet, and Paulina turned around. Sure enough, Colette, Nicky, and Pam entered from one of tunnels. The **Dark Fairies** were right behind them.

"They are **PRISONERS**," Paulina whispered.

"We have to think of something!" Violet whispered. "We have to help them!"

Will managed to push through and cut away the last **THREE** cables.

"**Done!**" he exclaimed.

"Move back!" Goldfire said. Then he stood up and spread his wings.

"Help our friends, please!" Violet begged him.

Goldfire nodded and took a **STEP** forward. At that moment, the fairies noticed the cut cables.

"The dragon is free!" they cried.

The three fairies launched an attack, *shooting* arrows and throwing **SHARP** flints at the dragon. But try as they might, nothing could put a dent in his golden armor. Instead, the flints bounced off the dragon EASILY.

In the meantime, Violet and Paulina had joined their friends, who were still prisoners of the fairies.

"**Let them go!**" Violet cried.

"Do you dare to challenge us?" the fairies replied, shooting the mouselets a look as **SHARP** as a glass shard.

"**STOP!**" Will shouted, stepping between them. "We aren't here to fight! We just want to help save the Crystal Kingdom!"

But the fairies ignored him. They advanced

Got the dragon!
He's free!

on Violet with a THREATENING look.

Will backed off in an effort to protect Paulina and Violet, but in doing so, he TRIPPED over a rock, and the GOLD DAGGER fell to the ground.

When the Dark Fairies saw the dagger, they gasped and backed off immediately.

One of the fairies stepped out in front of the others.

"Who gave you this dagger?" she asked.

"Arbor, Lord of the Golden Elves," Will replied.

"***Leave the dragon alone!***" the fairy instructed the others.

Will was surprised.

"Do you know Arbor?" he asked.

"Everyone in the Crystal Kingdom knows and respects Arbor," she replied. "The elves' gold is the purest, most precious

metal in the kingdom. Anyone who holds this dagger is our friend. We will not stand in your way."

Will and the Thea Sisters realized at once the true **POWER** of the dagger.

It wasn't a weapon but a symbol of *friendship* and **allegiance**.

Colette faced the fairies bravely.

"We aren't here to fight," she explained. "We have to free the dragon. He was put under an **EVIL SPELL**. The Crystal Kingdom will **shine** like it used to only when the spell is broken!"

"Very well," one of the fairies said at last. "You are all **free to go**!"

"Thank you," Colette said genuinely. Then she, Will, and the other Thea Sisters climbed onto Goldfire's back and left the Dark Caves **forever**.

Yay!
Let's go!

We made it!
Thank you, my friends!

IN THE CIRCLE OF LIGHT

As the dragon soared through the sky, the Thea Sisters recounted their good fortune.

"It was all thanks to the Golden Elves and the dagger," Colette replied.

"As soon as I can, I will visit Arbor to express my eternal gratitude," Goldfire said. "But first there is something very IMPORTANT I need to do."

"Find Esmeralda and break the spell," Violet answered for him.

They flew on for many miles, finally landing in the middle of a small valley.

"Where are we?" Will asked, looking at the WHITE desert that surrounded them.

"This is a very special place," the dragon

explained. "Those rocks outline the ancient CIRCLE OF INTENSE LIGHT. According to legend, the power of this light can break any evil spell."

From under his wings, Goldfire pulled a small, **brightly shining** gem.
Will and the mouselets watched, incredulous.

"But that's the **Star Amber**!" Paulina exclaimed in surprise.

"Yes, and Esmcralda is imprisoned inside," the dragon said **tenderly**.

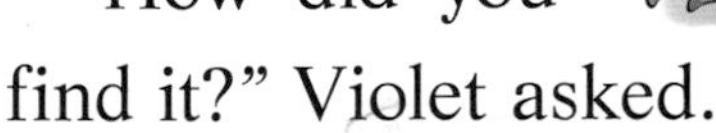

"How did you find it?" Violet asked.

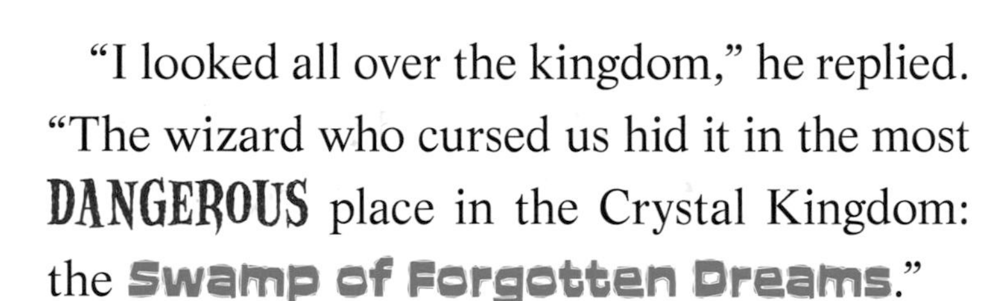

"I looked all over the kingdom," he replied. "The wizard who cursed us hid it in the most DANGEROUS place in the Crystal Kingdom: the Swamp of Forgotten Dreams."

"That sounds awful," Colette remarked.

"It is a truly TERRIBLE place," Goldfire agreed. "But my love for Esmeralda is stronger than fear, and it led me there to the Star Amber."

"How did you end up a prisoner in the DARK CAVES?" Paulina asked.

"On my way back from the swamp, the Dark Fairies captured me," the dragon explained.

"What's most important now is that you found the amber," Will said.

"Yes," Goldfire murmured as he held the stone close to his heart. "And now I will break the spell."

Suddenly, the CIRCLE OF INTENSE LIGHT appeared in the middle of the white rocks, as sparkly and pure as a diamond. The dragon took a step toward it, but then he hesitated.

Paulina gently placed a paw on his scales.

"REMEMBER: THE POWER OF YOUR LOVE FOR ESMERALDA IS STRONGER THAN FEAR!"

she reminded him.

With that, Goldfire tightened his hold on the Star Amber and flew bravely into the circle.

Immediately, a WALL OF LIGHT surrounded him, shielding him from the others. Will and the Thea Sisters waited, holding their breath. Then, just as suddenly as it had appeared, the light dimmed until

it faded away completely.

"Look!" Colette exclaimed. "Goldfire is gone!"

Instead, a brave **knight** had taken the dragon's place. A **beautiful** fairy stood beside him, holding his hand.

The mouselets recognized the couple. He looked different, but the knight had the same proud expression as **GOLDFIRE**.

"You did it!" Will exclaimed. "The spell is broken!"

The Thea Sisters cheered **happily**.

The knight took a bow and introduced himself.

"My name is **DIAMOND**, and this is **Esmeralda**, my bride-to-be."

The fairy looked at him **lovingly**. Then she turned to Will and the mouselets.

"My beloved knight and I have been

separated for **so long**," she said in a sweet voice. "But now, thanks to you, we are reunited!"

Suddenly, the white desert began to bloom

with crystals in all the COLORS of the rainbow!

"Look!" Nicky exclaimed. "The kingdom's beautiful crystals are back!"

"Diamond and Esmeralda's love broke the spell!" Paulina said with a sigh.

THE TALE OF DIAMOND AND ESMERALDA

Will and the Thea Sisters watched, mesmerized, as the incredible crystals continued to blossom like flowers all around them. Then Will reminded everyone of their **MISSION**.

"Mouselets, the first part of our mission is complete," Will said. "But now we must figure out how to awaken **Queen Tourmaline**."

"Perhaps I can help," Diamond said. "After all, I am responsible for most of the kingdom's damage."

"You didn't do it **on purpose**," Colette said sympathetically. "You were under an **EVIL SPELL**."

"True," Diamond replied. "But I haven't

told you the **entire** story yet."

"Does it have anything to do with the ***sleeping*** queen?" Paulina asked.

"Yes," Diamond said. "You already know the **evil wizard** sought revenge by turning me into a dragon and imprisoning me and Esmeralda in the **Twin Ambers**. But there is more to the tale . . ."

Will and the Thea Sisters looked at one another, **SURPRISED**.

"Go on," Will said simply.

"The wizard decided that once I became a dragon, I would **destroy** the same family I had protected as Hand of the King," Diamond continued.

"The **ROYAL** family!" Colette exclaimed.

"The wizard set the Sunlight Amber on the tip of a magic scepter," Diamond explained. "Then he disguised himself and presented it to the king as a gift. It was so beautiful the king decided to carry it with him always. But he did not know the wizard had cast an evil spell on the scepter: After **two hundred** full moons, the amber would crack, setting me free as a **dragon** to destroy the royal family — and the kingdom!"

"So that's the reason Queen Tourmaline

fell into a **deep sleep** when the amber shattered!" Paulina remarked.

"Yes," Diamond said, nodding regretfully. "Unfortunately, I was powerless to stop the evil spell since I was its **victim**, too."

"Perhaps there is something we can all do together," Pam suggested.

"We know there is a stone, the Sweet Awakening Gem, that can break the spell," Paulina added.

"The only problem is that we don't know where to **FIND** it!" Nicky said.

Diamond's face grew **SERIOUS** as he pondered the situation. Then Esmeralda, who had been quiet, spoke up suddenly.

"I am **familiar** with that gem!" she said.

"Do you know where we can find it?" Will asked eagerly.

"It's in the **Jade Jungle**," the fairy replied.

"How do you know about that **wild** place?" Diamond asked her, surprised.

"When I was a little girl, I would often **play** at the edge of the jungle," Esmeralda explained. "One day, I almost got lost among the plants and the *Jade Fairies* found me. They took care of me and showed me the way home. But before they said good-bye, they gave me this."

She showed them a charm pinned to her gown.

"During my time with the fairies, I heard the story of the Sweet Awakening Gem many times," she continued. "It's a special jade that can awaken anyone who is under an **evil** spell."

"So all we have to do now is get to the **Jade Jungle** and ask the fairies for the gem?" Pam asked.

"Unfortunately, it's not so easy," Esmeralda replied. "The Sweet Awakening Gem is guarded by a wolf named Fang."

"Do you know him?" Violet asked.

Esmeralda nodded.

"Do you think he would be willing to give us the gem?" Will asked hopefully.

"He will listen to us," Esmeralda replied. "But I can't say if he will help or not."

Then she turned and motioned for Will and the Thea Sisters to follow.

"Come," she said simply. "I will show you the way to the Jade Jungle."

And so the group of friends began the next leg of their journey.

To the jungle!

Let's go!
Follow me!

FANG THE WOLF

The Jade Jungle was a very bright and COLORFUL land. Majestic jade trees filled the horizon with their brilliant green leaves.

"This is one of the most extraordinary places in the entire Crystal Kingdom," Esmeralda explained. "These trees flourish only here, together in perfect HARMONY with the jungle."

The group of friends continued until they arrived at a little bridge over a sparkling blue river. Paulina was about to walk across when Esmeralda stopped her.

"**WAIT!**" the fairy cried in alarm.

Everyone stopped in surprise.

"What's wrong?" Diamond asked her.

"This isn't just any river," Esmeralda explained. "It's the border between Fang's territory and the rest of the Jade Jungle."

"So if we cross it, the **WOLF** could attack us?" Paulina asked, worried.

Esmeralda nodded.

"The wolf doesn't like intruders," she explained. "And he has been known

to become **AGGRESSIVE** with outsiders."

"So what should we do?" Will asked her.

"Let me go **FIRST**," the fairy replied.

"Esmeralda, it's **TOO DANGEROUS**!" Diamond said suddenly.

"Fang knows me," she said. "I'll be fine."

"But he hasn't seen you in a long time," the knight replied, worried. "What if he doesn't recognize you?"

"We have to take that **CHANCE**," the fairy said bravely. "I'm the only one who can face him."

"I think **Esmeralda** is right," Will said. "There's no other way."

"Okay," Diamond agreed at last. "But promise me you'll be careful!"

She smiled at him and nodded sweetly before she crossed the bridge.

The friends hid among the trees on the shore and, holding their breath, watched her walk away.

Esmeralda was confident as she stepped onto the opposite bank of the river. Suddenly, an animal jumped in front of her.

The fairy stopped, but she managed to remain calm.

On the other side, the Thea Sisters gasped in fear.

Diamond was about to run across the bridge to help, but Will held him back.

"We have to trust her," he said.

Meanwhile, Fang examined the fairy, his two rows of SHARP teeth visible. Suddenly, the animal GROWLED so loudly the leaves on the jade trees around the Thea Sisters trembled. But Esmeralda did not move a muscle.

"Who are you?" Fang growled. "How **DARE** you cross the border of this jungle?"

"It's me, Esmeralda," the fairy replied sweetly. "I know you, Fang. Don't you remember me?"

Upon hearing those words, the wolf's eyes sparkled brightly in recognition.

"Esmeralda, is that really you?" Fang asked softly.

"Yes," she replied. "It's really me, Fang "It's been such a long time since I played in these woods. Much has happened since then — some good things, and some bad."

She quickly told the wolf about the evil wizard and the amber, and about Diamond's rescue and of Will and the Thea Sisters' help.

"If I had been there to **PROTECT YOU**, none of this would have happened!" Fang said.

"Thank you," the fairy replied kindly.

"Your loyalty means so much. But now I am here on an important mission. Will you allow my friends to cross the **border**, too?"

The wolf nodded.

And so Will, the Thea Sisters, and Diamond walked across the bridge, watching the wolf anxiously.

"Esmerelda's friends are welcome here!"

Fang said as soon as they were across. Then he led them into his den.

Follow me . . .

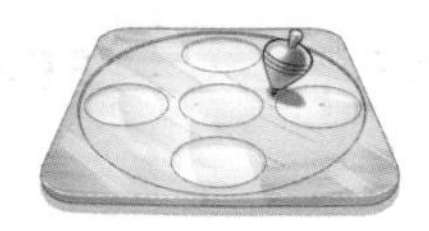

THE JADE QUADRANT

To get to the wolf's den, the group had to go through a hidden hole dug out from the roots of a large tree. At the end of the **tunnel**, the friends entered a large room that was barely lit by sunlight streaming in from one tiny opening.

"What brings you to the Jade Jungle?" Fang wanted to know. He offered his guests a place to sit on small tree stumps.

"We need your help," Esmeralda replied. "A **wizard** cast an evil spell over the Crystal Kingdom. Our dear queen has fallen into a deep sleep."

"We went to the Query Quartz and discovered only one thing can wake her: the

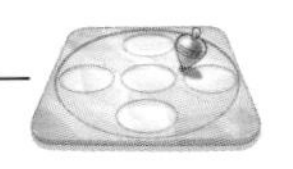

Sweet Awakening Gem!" Paulina added.

Fang looked at Esmeralda, astonished.

"You know very well that the gem cannot leave the jungle," he said severely.

"Yes, I know the rules," the fairy replied. "But this is a **VERY SERIOUS** situation! The entire kingdom is in **DANGER**!"

The wolf considered their case. Finally, he spoke.

"Very well, then," he agreed. "But you have to pass some tests."

"What do you mean?" Will asked.

"Only the one who has proven his or her bravery can receive the gem," Fang explained. "Otherwise it will lose its powers once it is **removed** from the jungle."

"We are not afraid," Diamond replied.

The **WOLF** gestured for the group of friends to follow him to a small side cave. A **LARGE** stone disk rested on the floor of the cave, LIT by the fire.

"This is the **Jade Quadrant**," the wolf explained. "It is one of the most ancient stones in the entire kingdom. There is a map etched on it."

Fang pointed to an object resting next to the quadrant and asked Diamond to pick it up and show it to the others.

"The **spinning top** will determine the tests you will have to perform," Fang explained.

Diamond placed the top on the slab of stone and made it **spin**. It moved quickly from one side of the map to the other. Finally, it dropped.

"It stopped on the **Crystal Woods**," Fang said. "This is your **FIRST task**: You must go the woods and climb the tallest tree. At

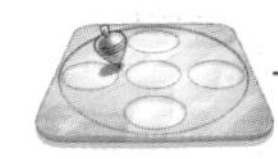

the **TOP** you will find a very special **FRUIT** made of alabaster stone. You will pick the fruit and bring it back here to me."

"That doesn't seem too hard," Nicky blurted out.

But Fang shook his head.

"This isn't a normal piece of fruit," the wolf said. "There's only **one way** to pluck it from the tree: It will be part of your test to figure that out."

"Okay," Diamond replied. "We understand the **FIRST** test. What comes next?"

"It's your turn now, traveler," Fang said to Will. He picked up the top and spun it on the quadrant. The top **twirled** and **twirled** across the surface while the Thea Sisters looked on nervously. Finally, it fell.

"It stopped on the **RUBY CAVES**," Fang said.

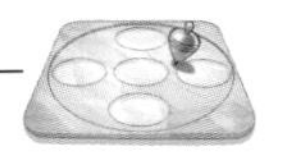

"The stones on Queen Tourmaline's bracelet come from there," Colette recalled immediately.

The wolf nodded.

"This is your second task," he said. "The Ruby Caves are one of the most amazing places in the kingdom. You must find the **BLOOD RUBY**. Its beauty is unmatched. It will be right in the middle of the caves."

"Will it be difficult?" Will asked.

"Yes," Fang replied. "Only the Ruby Fairies can navigate the tunnels and passageways. Anyone who tries to get through the caves without their help is **LOST FOREVER**."

"Can you tell us what makes these caves so tricky?" Will asked.

"They are made up of thousands of very confusing tunnels, just like a maze," the wolf explained.

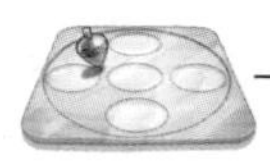

"I think it might be best if we SPLIT UP," Will suggested.

"I agree," Diamond said solemnly.

They quickly decided that Will, Colette, Paulina, and Esmeralda would go to the **RUBY CAVES**, while the others would

travel to the **Crystal Woods**.

"Thank you, Fang," Esmeralda told the wolf.

He smiled at them.

"Go prove your courage and bravery," he said encouragingly.

TO THE RUBY CAVES

Will, Colette, Paulina, and Esmeralda started heading south. Soon the Jade Jungle was behind them and they were briskly walking toward their destination: the **RUBY CAVES**.

"Are you afraid of getting lost in the caves?" Paulina asked Esmerelda.

"A little bit, but I have faith that we'll make it!" she replied.

"Esmeralda is right, mouselets!" Will agreed. "*We have to believe in ourselves!*"

As they walked, the landscape around

them changed. Soon the jungle trees had been replaced by flat **GREEN GRASS**.

Colette studied the blades of grass, fascinated: Each one was threaded with hundreds of tiny, **delicate** green pearls.

"Look at how they **glow** in the sunlight!" she exclaimed in delight.

As Colette walked through a patch of

the sparkling grass, dozens of COLORFUL BUTTERFLIES suddenly soared up from the grass into the sky.

"Look!" She gasped. "They have crystal wings!"

"The CRYSTAL KINGDOM never fails to surprise us!" Will remarked.

The group continued along, with Paulina checking the map from the Crystal Fairies every so often.

"We should be close," she said.

"Look over there!" Esmeralda exclaimed.

The friends saw a large vine climbing up the face of some rocks. Its branches were full of scarlet leaves, which covered the entrance to a cave.

"This must be it," Paulina said hopefully. "It doesn't look very DANGEROUS . . ."

"Still, we should be careful," Esmeralda

warned. "Don't be fooled. Fang said these caves could be very TRICKY."

"Esmeralda is right," Will agreed. "Let's go **slowly** and **carefully**. Hopefully we'll find a CLUE as to how we find the **middle** of the cave."

They entered the cave and walked a long

way. The tunnel seemed to be **endless**. Finally, the group came to a CROSSROAD.

"Which way should we go?" Paulina wondered.

"I am SO SORRY," Esmeralda replied, confused. "I feel **HELPLESS**. I'm afraid I

don't know my way around in here."

"It's okay," Will reassured her. "We'll find a way — together!"

"So what do you suggest now?" Colette asked her friends.

"Let's go RIGHT," Paulina suggested. "It worked at the **Blue Topaz**!"

Everyone agreed, and they turned down the tunnel to the right and continued on their journey. Colette, Paulina, Will, and Esmeralda came across many more forks in the road and followed MYSTERIOUS uphill and downhill paths. Suddenly, Paulina confirmed their worst fear.

"**OH NO!**" she squeaked. "**WE ALREADY WALKED THIS WAY!**"

"Are you sure?" Colette asked.

"Yes," Paulina replied. "I noticed those **five stones** arranged in the shape of a

star when we passed this spot earlier."

"That was clever," Will complimented her. "But I'm afraid we're still in a bad spot."

"Right," Colette agreed, nodding. "It seems we're **LOST**!"

WHEN YOU LEAST EXPECT IT . . .

Esmeralda, Will, and the mouselets were in trouble. They kept walking for a little bit longer, taking turns they hadn't picked the **FIRST** time around. Still, they kept finding themselves in the same place **again**!

"We're walking in **circles**," Colette said, discouraged.

"The only thing we can do is try to figure out how these tunnels are designed," Paulina said. "It's like a **puzzle**. There has to be a **logical** explanation."

"Fang said there is no **PATTERN**." Esmerelda sighed. "Only the fairies can walk around here and not get **lost**."

"Perhaps there are some *MARKS* on the

walls," Paulina speculated, carefully checking the rocks. Esmeralda and Colette looked for marks or signs, too, with no **luck**.

Suddenly, Colette saw something out of the corner of her eye.

"Hey," she cried, pointing her paw. "I just saw something over there! It looked like the **SHADOW** of someone moving through the caves. Maybe someone's hiding behind that **ROCK**."

Will stepped forward to take a look.

"Wait!" Esmeralda stopped him. "The Ruby Fairies are **very shy**. If it is indeed one of them, she might be scared off, and our chance for help will **disappear** with her. Let me go."

Esmeralda moved very slowly, inching her way closer to the rock where Colette had pointed.

"Ruby Fairy," she whispered softly. "Please do not be afraid. I am a Crystal Fairy, and I come in **peace**."

There was no reply.

"You can **trust me**," Esmeralda pressed gently. "Please come out."

Slowly, a fairy with curly **ruby-red** hair emerged from behind the rock.

"What is your name?" Esmeralda asked her.

"I am called Rubix," she replied. Then she glanced at Will, Colette, and Paulina. "We do not usually have visitors here. What brings you to the caves?"

"Dear fairy, we are here on a very **IMPORTANT** mission," Colette replied.

"We are having a hard time finding our way through the tunnels of the Ruby Caves," Paulina went on. "I'm afraid we are lost."

"You shouldn't be here," Rubix replied.

"But we need the **BLOOD RUBY**," Will explained.

Rubix **shook** her head.

"That is impossible," she said. "No one can take the ruby."

"But we need it for **Queen Tourmaline**!" Will persisted.

"Why didn't the queen come here herself, then?" the fairy asked.

"She is in a **deep sleep**," Paulina replied. "An evil wizard cast a spell on her, and no one has been able to **WAKE** her."

Rubix was silent for a moment as she studied them again. Finally, she spoke. "It would be best if you leave," she said. "Now."

"Please," Esmeralda pleaded with the fairy. "I beg of you. Please help us!"

At that moment, Rubix noticed the BRACELET Esmeralda was wearing on her wrist. She gasped.

"That bracelet!" Rubix exclaimed, tears in her eyes. "You must be Esmeralda!"

"Have we met before?" Esmeralda asked, SURPRISED.

"A long time ago," Rubix explained. "I was just a little girl, but you saved my life!"

"Now I remember!" Esmeralda exclaimed. "You were caught in a STORM and you became injured. I helped you, but I never learned your name. You were too scared to utter a word."

"That's right," Rubix replied, nodding.

"A lot has happened since then," Esmeralda continued. "The Crystal Kingdom is in

grave danger. We need to wake the queen. Help us, please!"

The fairy nodded.

"I will," she said simply. "As you once helped me, I will help you. I can see your intentions are pure."

"**THANK YOU!**" Colette and Paulina exclaimed **happily**.

"We are so grateful," Esmeralda added, smiling at Rubix.

THE RED STRING

Now that Rubix was ***guiding*** them through the caves, Esmeralda, Will, Paulina, and Colette felt more confident.

Suddenly, Rubix stopped and bent down

in the middle of the tunnel. She began to dig in the **dark sand** at her feet.

"What are you doing?" Esmeralda asked, confused.

"I am looking for the **red string**," Rubix explained.

"What's that?" Colette asked, intrigued.

"It's an unbreakable string that winds through the different tunnels of the Ruby Caves and leads all the way to the center," she replied. "It's old. The very first fairies who lived here WOVE it by using thousands of small ruby flecks."

"It's gorgeous!" Colette remarked, looking at it closely.

"Here, hold the thread while you walk," Rubix said, smiling. "Legend says it gives courage and STRENGTH to anyone who is on a difficult mission."

The group of friends continued through one long tunnel after another.

"We would have never made it without you and the red string," Paulina told Rubix. "Thank you so much!"

At that moment, the fairy stopped in front of a bright, ruby-encrusted gate.

“Here we are!” she declared. “This is the center of the Ruby Caves.”

Will, Esmeralda, Colette, and Paulina were elated. The fairy raised her right hand and removed her necklace. A key hung from the chain. Rubix carefully slid it into the gate’s keyhole. A moment later, the gate CREAKED open slowly.

Welcome, my friends!
Incredible!

How beautiful!

"Follow me," the fairy told them.

They were squeakless at what they saw on the other side of the gate. **Shimmering** ruby-red stalactites hung from the ceiling above a small village, which sat on the banks of a crystal-blue river.

"Pretty, isn't it?" Rubix asked when she saw how dazzled her guests were by the scenery.

"I've never seen anything like this," Colette remarked.

"What an amazing place!" Will said.

"Thank you," Rubix replied, smiling. Then she pointed to crystal stairs at the back of the cave. "The **BLOOD RUBY** is up there."

Will, Colette, Paulina, and Esmeralda watched as she climbed all the way up to the pedestal. Then she delicately lifted the **RUBY** and carried it back down, where she presented it to Esmeralda.

"**Thank you!**" Colette exclaimed. "We are so grateful."

"Now we have to get back to the **Jade Jungle**!" Paulina reminded them. "It will be a long journey."

"Probably not as long as you might think . . ." Rubix said, smiling

cryptically. "Come with me." She led Will, Esmeralda, Paulina, and Colette to the edge of the crystal-blue **water**.

"This **underground river** leads all the way to the Jade Jungle," she explained.

"Wow!" Colette cried. "We should have taken it on the way here!"

"You can sail only from the village to the jungle, not the other way around," Rubix said. "Only the **Ruby Fairies** know about it.

"I must ask you to keep it a SECRET. This way we can continue to protect our caves."

"Of course," Esmeralda, Will, Paulina, and

Colette agreed quickly. "We won't tell anyone."

Rubix showed them small, beautiful boats that had been carved from red crystals.

"When you arrive at your destination, the boats will dissolve in the water and disappear," Rubix explained. "That way our SECRET will be safe."

"Wow!" Paulina exclaimed in awe. "That's incredible."

The fairy smiled.

"Now go," she said, bidding them farewell. "Good luck!"

Will, Esmeralda, Paulina, and Colette each got on a boat. Then they pushed off and sailed down the river and out of the mysterious and magical Ruby Caves forever.

TO THE CRYSTAL WOODS

While the first group of friends was leaving the Ruby Caves and sailing on the underground river, Diamond, Violet, Pamela, and Nicky were heading west, toward the **Crystal Woods**.

The group quickly arrived in the spectacular **BLUE ONYX VALLEY**.

"Holey cheese, what an INCREDIBLE color!" Pamela exclaimed when she saw the blue land before her.

"Look at those *flowers* growing among

those crystal-blue stones," Violet remarked.

"It doesn't look like this part of the Crystal Kingdom sustained any **damage**," Pam said as she took in the landscape.

"No, it doesn't look like it," Diamond confirmed quietly.

Pam immediately realized she might have hurt Diamond's feelings.

"I'm so sorry!" she exclaimed. "That wasn't very sensitive of me. I hope I wasn't hurtful. We all know everything happened because of the **evil spell** cast by the wizard."

"I know," Diamond said sadly. "Still, the Crystal Kingdom was almost destroyed forever because of me. It's hard not to feel guilty."

"What's important now is that the spell has been broken and you and Esmeralda are back together," Violet said comfortingly.

"And you're working hard to make **amends**," Nicky added. "We need your help to find the Alabaster Fruit so we can get the Sweet Awakening Gem and save the queen."

"Then everything will be okay," Pam said, **smiling**.

They continued walking through the valley until they arrived in the **Crystal Woods**.

"Wow!" Nicky said as she reached out to touch

a beautiful crystal-blue tree. "It's so cold!"

"It's such a strange tree," Violet mused, intrigued. "It's almost as if you can see THROUGH it."

"Could the tree we're looking for be near here?" Pam asked Diamond.

"It's the tallest tree," Diamond replied. "So we should be able to recognize it."

They looked around, but the leaves of the trees surrounding them were TOO THICK for them to see very much.

"It's hard to tell," Violet said, "but I don't see any sign of the Alabaster Fruit Tree."

"Wait!" Pam said suddenly. "Do you hear that? It sounds like RATTLING GLASS . . ."

Nicky stepped into some CRYSTAL BUSHES, pushing the branches aside.

"Whoa," she said. "Mouselets, you should come take a LOOK at this . . ."

Wow!
That sound!

It's enormouse!

Diamond, Violet, and Pam hurried over. When they reached the clearing on the other side of the bushes, they were squeakless.

They were standing in front of the biggest and tallest TREE they had ever seen. Its rich foliage was BRIGHT in the sunlight, and its **crystal leaves** fluttered in the wind, making a sound like a thousand small bells ringing.

Diamond smiled.

"I think we found it," he said.

"IT'S THE ALABASTER FRUIT TREE!"

THE ALABASTER FRUIT

Diamond and the mouselets stood at the foot of the tree and looked **UP**.

"Holey cheese, is it **TALL**!" Nicky exclaimed.

"I think the only way to reach the fruit is to climb to the top," Diamond replied, and he prepared to start.

But Nicky **STOPPED** him.

"You don't have to climb alone," she said.

"It's the least I can do for my kingdom, considering all the **DESTRUCTION** I have caused," the knight replied.

"Still, I'm coming with you!" Nicky said firmly. "I'm an **expert climber**, and we can work together up there!"

"Okay," Diamond replied, *graciously*

accepting his friend's help. "Let's go, then!"

"We'll have to be very cautious," Nicky said wisely as she grabbed a rope and TIED it around her waist. Diamond did the same.

"Ready?" Diamond asked Nicky once they both had their safety gear on.

"Yes!" Nicky said. "We'd better start CLIMBING. It could take a while to get to the top."

"How will you pick the fruit?" Violet asked, worried.

"I guess we'll figure it out once we get there," Diamond replied. "We'll have to get the tree to trust us enough to give us the fruit!"

Violet and Pam gave

them encouraging hugs and wished them **good luck**. Then the two friends started to climb.

The tree trunk was larger and more **SLIPPERY** than they expected. Thankfully, there were branches staggered at different heights, and Diamond and Nicky were able to grab them and slowly pull themselves up the tree.

"This climb seems never ending," Nicky puffed as she took a break to rest.

"It looks like we're only about HALFWAY there," Diamond said. "At least we can start to see the **TOP**!"

The higher they **climbed**, the more **tired** they became.

Still, they pressed on. The most important goal was to reach the **FRUIT**. Slowly, one step after another, they finally made their

way to the top.

"**There it is!**" Nicky exclaimed, relieved.

She could finally see the precious **ALABASTER FRUIT**. It looked slightly bigger than an apple, with **red** skin streaked by white. "I'll try to pick it," Nicky said.

Nicky reached out and **GRABBED** the fruit with her paw. Then she tugged at it gently, but

it wouldn't budge. She twisted and turned the fruit and tried pulling HARDER, but it held tight.

"It feels like it's GLUED on," she remarked.

"Let me try," Diamond said.

The knight turned the fruit and pulled, then turned it the other way and pulled again. Still, he had **no luck** removing it.

"It's more difficult than I thought," he acknowledged. "It almost feels like it's resisting."

Suddenly, Nicky had an idea. She placed her open paw right below the fruit and waited patiently. Diamond watched her quietly.

Just as Nicky was about to give up, sure that her **hunch** had been wrong, something happened.

"***IT'S COMING OFF!***" Diamond gasped.

Nicky remained still and focused her

attention and energy on the precious fruit. A few moments later, the fruit fell into her paw.

"It worked!" she exclaimed happily.

"What did you do?" the knight asked, curious.

"I was reminded of some fruit that grows in Australia, where I'm from," Nicky explained. "Even though the fruit looks tough, it's actually very delicate. If it is picked the wrong way, the fruit is ruined. I thought maybe it was the same for the Alabaster Fruit."

"Amazing," Diamond replied. "I would have never thought of that!"

"You gave me the idea," Nicky said. "I know force isn't allowed in the Crystal Woods. So instead, I was gentle and patient."

"Great job," Diamond congratulated her.

"Now let's get back to the others!"

Climbing down was much easier, and they were back on the ground in no time.

"How did it go?" Violet asked eagerly when she saw her friends.

Nicky smiled and held out her paw.

"Here's the ALABASTER FRUIT!" she said happily.

"Nicky was absolutely fantastic!" Diamond complimented her.

Violet and Pam hugged their friend proudly. Then they admired the strange fruit. Finally, the group headed back to the Jade Jungle together.

TOGETHER AGAIN

While Diamond, Nicky, Violet, and Pam were walking back, Will, Esmeralda, Colette, and Paulina arrived in the Jade Jungle.

"Here we are!" Will exclaimed as they climbed out of the SCARLET BOATS and watched in wonder as they magically disappeared.

"I wonder if the others are back yet," Esmeralda asked.

"Let's hurry back to Fang, and we'll find out," Will said, and the group headed straight for the WOLF'S DEN.

"You're back!" Fang exclaimed.

"Yes, and we have the **BLOOD RUBY**," Will replied, pleased.

"Well done," the wolf congratulated them. "That was not an easy **task**."

At that moment, they heard voices coming from the forest. Soon they saw Diamond, Pam, Violet, and Nicky emerge from the woods.

"Mouselets, you're back, too!" Colette said, happy to see her friends again.

"It went really well!" Pam exclaimed. "Diamond and Nicky were amazing: They climbed to the top of the tree and managed to pick the **ALABASTER FRUIT**!"

Will turned toward Fang.

"What next?" he asked the wolf eagerly.

"Since you passed the tests, all that is left is for you to bring the two stones to the *Jade Fairies*," Fang said. "They will give you what you are looking for."

Without waiting for a reply, the wolf led

the group of friends to the most beautiful and inaccessible part of the jungle: **Jade Village**.

We're going to the Jade Fairies!

A SURPRISE WITH WINGS

When they arrived at their destination, Will and the Thea Sisters couldn't believe their eyes. It was a beautiful VILLAGE, completely surrounded by mountains and accessible via a carved WOODEN BRIDGE.

"What a dreamy place," Paulina remarked as they crossed the bridge, which spanned a shimmering *emerald-green river*.

On the other side of the bridge, **two fairies** welcomed them with a friendly smile.

"How nice to see you, Fang," the first one said.

"Welcome," the second one added in a

clear, melodic voice. "What can we do for you and your friends?"

"We would like to meet with Fairy Selenite," the wolf told them.

"Come with us," the first fairy replied. Then she led the group of friends through Jade Village.

"This place sparkles like a precious piece of jewelry," Pamela remarked.

"And look at these lovely little cottages!" Violet added.

The two fairies stopped in front of the largest cottage.

One of the fairies stepped inside. She emerged again a moment later.

"Fairy Selenite has agreed to see you," she told them. "Come."

The group followed the fairy inside. There, another fairy was seated on an intricately

This way!

It sparkles like a piece of jewelry!
Amazing!
Look at these cottages!

carved wooden throne, a thin bejeweled crown on her head. Fang kneeled before her, and the others quickly followed his example and did the same.

"Welcome, travelers," Selenite greeted them. Then she turned and signaled to another fairy, who flew over to them with a tray full of cupcakes.

"Please, help yourselves, my dear guests," Selenite said. "You must be tired and very hungry."

Pam didn't hesitate. She quickly took a cupcake covered in sparkling pale-green CREAM.

"Yum!" she exclaimed. Her friends helped themselves to the delicious-looking treats as well.

"I am delighted you like them," Selenite replied. "These are special Jade Village

cupcakes, based on an old recipe. They are filled with **fruit** that grows only here, in our woods."

Pam finished her cupcake in one bite.

"Now, tell me, what brings you here?" Selenite asked Fang and the Thea Sisters.

"We are here because a wizard cast an **evil spell** over the Crystal Kingdom," Fang began. "Queen Tourmaline has fallen into a **deep sleep** and no one has been able to wake her."

"I see," Selenite replied, nodding. "So you are here for the Sweet Awakening Gem."

The wolf nodded in reply.

"Fang, you know the Jade Jungle **RULES**," Selenite said firmly.

"Of course," the wolf replied.

Then he turned to Diamond and Esmeralda and asked them to show Selenite the **BLOOD**

RUBY and the **ALABASTER FRUIT**.

The fairy recognized both stones and nodded in acknowledgement.

"You have shown a great deal of **courage**," Selenite remarked. "I will give you the gem."

She rose from her throne and opened a

large trunk that was sitting nearby. She removed the Sweet Awakening Gem and showed it to the group of friends.

"I hope you understand just how special this is," she said.

Selenite handed the gem to Will.

At the same time, Diamond and Esmeralda

handed the **BLOOD RUBY** and the **ALABASTER FRUIT** to two other fairies.

"We thank you from the bottoms of our hearts, Selenite," Will said. "Now we have to get back to Joystone Castle: **Queen Tourmaline** needs us!"

"There's one thing you should know," Selenite said suddenly. "The gem's **power** will be activated only when it is placed on the queen's heart."

"Thank you!" Colette replied. "We'll remember."

Then a group of fairies approached Will and the Thea Sisters. Each fairy was holding a silver string with a heart-shaped **jade pendant**.

"These necklaces are for you," one of the fairies explained. "The charms are made of the purest jade and will protect you on the

rest of your journey."

Then she tied the **precious pendant** around Colette's neck. The other fairies did the same for the remaining Thea Sisters.

"Thank you," Colette exclaimed, touched by the fairy's gift. "It's so beautiful!"

Then Selenite walked them out of the cottage.

"The queen's **destiny** is in your hands now," she said. Then she blew a small whistle and a **crystal-clear sound** echoed all around. A moment later, eight white WINGED HORSES appeared right before the group of travelers.

"They will take

you to **Joystone Castle**," Selenite told the Thea Sisters and their friends.

In the meantime, Fang bid Esmeralda farewell.

"I was so happy to see you again," the wolf said.

"*Thank you for everything*," Esmeralda replied, hugging the creature warmly.

"Enjoy your journey!" the fairies exclaimed.

Then they stood to the side, waving at the group of travelers until the WINGED HORSES disappeared on the horizon.

RETURN TO JOYSTONE CASTLE

Will, the Thea Sisters, and their fairy friends flew to **Joystone Castle** as quickly as they could.

"The Jade Fairies were very kind to ask the winged horses to fly us here," Paulina said as her horse landed gently in the castle's **gardens**.

"It would have taken us much longer to get here if they hadn't," Colette said.

"It's not over yet, though," Will said.

"Yes, we still need to wake the queen!" Nicky agreed.

The Thea Sisters and their friends thanked the horses and hurried into the castle.

"You're back!" Agatha welcomed them

warmly. Then she saw Esmeralda and Diamond, and her eyes filled with TEARS.

"Is it really you?" she asked, incredulous.

"Yes!" Esmeralda replied, running to hug her friend. "We're home at last!"

"What happened?" Agatha asked. "I hadn't heard from you in such a long time!"

Esmeralda quickly told her about the evil wizard's spell and the Twin Ambers.

In the meantime, more fairies came to listen to the story.

"Diamond, YOU were the dragon?" Galena asked, stunned.

The knight hung his head sadly.

"Yes," he confirmed. "It was me. You have no idea how badly I feel about all the DAMAGE I caused. But there was nothing I could do — the wizard's spell was TOO POWERFUL!"

"I'm so sorry," Agatha said, sighing. "You've had to go through so much. I'm sure it wasn't easy."

"The only thing that matters now is that we wake Queen Tourmaline."

Will opened his backpack and removed the Sweet Awakening Gem. The fairies gasped when they saw it.

"You did it!" Agatha said. "Let's take it to the queen right away."

When the group entered Tourmaline's bedroom, she was lying on her bed, her eyes closed. Esmeralda walked over and took her hand.

"My dear queen, your sweet laughter will fill the castle again soon," the fairy said.

"I think you should do it," Will said, handing the gem to Esmeralda.

The fairy took the gem and closed her eyes, focusing on only one wish: for the queen to wake up from her **deep sleep**. Then she gently put the gem on Tourmaline's **heart**. The room was completely silent.

Everyone waited for the gem's **POWER** to take hold. After a few long moments, something started happening: The queen's eyelashes fluttered and she **slowly** opened her eyes.

It took a moment for **Queen Tourmaline** to take in all the fairies standing around her.

"What happened?" she asked at last. "Esmeralda and Diamond: You're **FINALLY** back!"

"Your Highness, we are so **happy** you're well!" Agatha exclaimed.

"I don't understand . . ." the queen said slowly. "My **last memory** is of the scepter shattering on the floor and then darkness filling the room. After that, I can recall **NOTHING** at all . . ."

Diamond told her everything that had happened, with Esmeralda, Will, and the

Thea Sisters filling in some of the details.

The queen listened intently.

At the end of the story, Queen Tourmaline looked pensive.

"The Crystal Kingdom went through a very **difficult** time," she said. "But you all stepped up to face the **challenge** with courage and determination. I thank you all from the bottom of my heart. I am so very proud of my people!"

"All hail the queen!" the fairies replied **joyfully**.

Then Queen Tourmaline addressed Will and the Thea Sisters.

"Thank you for everything you've done for us," she said. "Without your help, our beloved CRYSTAL KINGDOM would no longer exist."

"You are very welcome, Your Highness," Will replied. "An **amazing** world like this must be protected!"

FAIRIES FOR A DAY

Now that the queen was awake, Joystone Castle was in full celebration mode. In fact, the entire Crystal Kingdom was lively again.

"You did a really great job, mouselets!" Will congratulated them.

The Thea Sisters smiled, pleased that they had been able to make a difference.

"It's too bad we have to leave so soon," Violet said sadly.

At that moment, Esmeralda walked over.

"I have amazing news!" she told them excitedly.

"What is it?" Nicky asked, eager to find out why the fairy's eyes were TWINKLING so brightly.

"Queen Tourmaline decided to celebrate by throwing a **BIG** party: You're all invited to

the Crystal Kingdom's Grand Ball!"

She handed them six handwritten cards, which had been decorated with colorful fairy dust.

"How *exquisite*!" Colette gasped when she saw the invitation.

"We would be honored to attend the ball!" Paulina cried.

Esmeralda twirled around in excitement.

"I'm so glad you'll come!" the fairy exclaimed.

"And we're thrilled, too!" Colette said. She thought of the colorful decorations, delicious **food**, and elegant **gowns** the fairies would surely display for the occasion.

"All the creatures in the Crystal Kingdom will attend this special event," Esmeralda explained.

"The Golden Elves, too?" Nicky asked.

"Of course!" Esmeralda replied with a wink. "I'm sure Arbor was one of the first ones invited."

"What do you mean?" Paulina asked.

"The queen and Arbor are in **love**," Esmeralda whispered. "But long ago, the elves needed Arbor to help them protect the Eternal Woods. So he agreed to **sacrifice** his love for the queen to protect his own people."

"How sad!" Violet remarked.

"I'm sure they'll be **happy** to see each other again at the ball after all this time," Colette added wistfully.

"Yes," Esmeralda agreed, smiling. "And now we must get ready for the dance. I want

to show you a very special place . . ."

The Thea Sisters followed the fairy through the castle's glimmering hallways to a round room filled with light.

"This is the fairies' DRESSING room," she said, inviting them in. "There are tiaras, earrings, bracelets, gowns, shoes, and bags, all decorated with precious crystals!"

The five friends were squeakless. They were mesmerized by the racks of gorgeous dresses, shelves of sparkling shoes, and closets full of elegant accessories.

"I've never seen anything like this!"

Colette exclaimed, her eyes bright with excitement.

"Please choose anything you would like to wear for the ball," Esmeralda told them.

"Wow! Really?!" Violet exclaimed.

Wow!
Oooh!
This is the dressing room!
It's like a dream!

"We don't know how to thank you, Esmeralda," Paulina chimed in. "This **jewelry** is amazing!"

Colette immediately tried on a **necklace** in her favorite colors: white, gold, pink, and sapphire.

"Look!" she said, modeling for her friends.

"That's amazing," Nicky said in response. "It looks beautiful on you."

"Wow!" Violet agreed.

"It would look great with these **diamond-encrusted shoes**," Paulina suggested.

"Perfect!" Colette said.

"These **gowns** are each more gorgeous than the last!" Pamela said as she looked through the elegant dresses in the **closet**.

"Choosing one won't be **easy**," Nicky agreed.

"What do you think of this one?" Violet

asked as she pulled out a gown covered in **tiny pearls**.

"I love it!" Nicky said.

The Thea Sisters happily tried on jewelry and accessories until each one of them found something perfect to wear to the ***Grand Ball***.

THE GRAND BALL

Just a few hours later, Joystone Castle had been decorated with **colorful gems** and *pearl flowers*. It looked more beautiful and welcoming than ever.

As soon as they were dressed for the dance, the Thea Sisters walked into the ballroom. **Esmeralda** and **DIAMOND** were standing right by the door, waiting for them.

"***You look stunning!***" the fairy exclaimed when she saw them.

"You look breathtaking, as well!" the mouselets replied, admiring the fairy and her knight.

"Esmeralda is right," Will said, joining his friends. "**YOU FIVE LOOK TRULY RADIANT!**"

"Thank you, Will," Colette replied. "And you look very **HANDSOME**."

The ballroom was crowded with fairies and elves, all wearing the most **beautiful** clothes and jewelry the mouselets had ever seen.

The group of friends paid their respects to **Queen Tourmaline**, who was no doubt the most elegant fairy there. She was wearing a long **CRYSTAL-ENCRUSTED** evening gown.

"Your Highness, please allow us to thank you for inviting us to this **beautiful** party," Will said, taking a bow.

"And thank you for lending us these **beautiful clothes**!" Colette went on.

"It is an **honor** to have you here," Queen Tourmaline replied.

"A lot of guests are here already," Paulina remarked.

"Yes, almost everyone is here," the queen replied as she glanced around the room as if looking for someone. The mouselets heard a note of **sadness** in her voice.

At that moment, a valet announced the arrival of more guests.

"The Golden Elves have arrived, Queen Tourmaline," the valet called. "Led by their lord, **Arbor the Brave**!"

A group of elves wearing elegant **golden** capes walked into the room. Arbor was at the head of the group, walking proudly. He approached Queen Tourmaline immediately. Then he bowed and **kissed** her hand.

For a moment, the queen seemed stunned.

"You are even more **beautiful** than I remember," Arbor said softly.

Welcome back, Your Highness!

"It's so great to see you," the queen replied, **happy** tears in her eyes.

The orchestra began to play a lovely tune, and Arbor invited the queen to dance. A moment later, the ball had officially begun!

THE CRYSTAL DOLPHINS

The next morning, the Thea Sisters prepared to head home.

They stopped to say **good-bye** to Queen Tourmaline.

"I'll never forget everything you did for the **CRYSTAL KINGDOM** and for me," she told them sincerely. "I hope you will come back to visit one day."

"We hope so, too!" Violet replied.

"The **Royal Crystal Dolphins** will take you back to the Sapphire Sea," Queen Tourmaline said.

Then Esmeralda led them to the Semi-Precious Stones Spring. Six **beautiful** dolphins were waiting for them there. The

Thea Sisters hugged the fairy tenderly. Then they climbed onto the crystal dolphins.

The creatures swam along a secret canal that led all the way back to the beach where their **adventure** had begun.

They thanked the animals and headed to

the **Crystal Elevator**. Then Will played a few notes of the magic song that would ***transport*** them home. A few moments later, the elevator had returned the group to the **SEVEN ROSES UNIT**.

PRECIOUS MEMORIES

Back in the Seven Roses Unit, Will congratulated the Thea Sisters again for a job well done.

"I'm really **PROUD** of all of you," Will said. "You can return to Mouseford right away on our helicopter. That way you can finally go on your well-deserved **vacations**!"

"Woo-hoo!" Colette exclaimed. "The Crystal Kingdom was incredible, but I can't wait to rest on the **beach**."

As the five mice boarded the helicopter, a small notebook fell out of Will's **backpack**. He picked it up.

"What's this?" he wondered.

"It looks like a **photo album**," Paulina replied.

"How wonderful!" Colette said, admiring the cover, which was decorated with **colorful crystals**.

Will opened it and read the dedication:

Dear friends,
These drawings are made with crystal paints.
We hope this gift will help you remember us.
Love,
Queen Tourmaline and the Crystal Fairies

"What a *lovely* gesture!" Violet said, teary-eyed.

"Look at these beautiful images!" Colette said as she flipped through the album. There were pictures of the Emerald Forest, the Ruby Caves, Jade Village, Joystone Castle, and all the other **amazing places** the mouselets had visited during their mission in the CRYSTAL KINGDOM.

"Thank you for all your help," Will said gratefully. "Now I hope you'll enjoy your **TIME OFF**!"

The mouselets followed Will to the helicopter that would take them back to Mouseford Academy.

After a smooth, relaxing flight home, it was time for the five friends to say good-bye to Will.

The mouselets looked up at the STARRY NIGHT SKY and hugged one another tightly as they set paw on Whale Island again. The Moon was brightening the sky like a precious CRYSTAL.

"Good-bye!" the mouselets called as their friend boarded the helicopter.

"See you on the next MISSION!" came Will's reply.

Don't miss any of these exciting Thea Sisters adventures!

Thea Stilton and the Dragon's Code

Thea Stilton and the Mountain of Fire

Thea Stilton and the Ghost of the Shipwreck

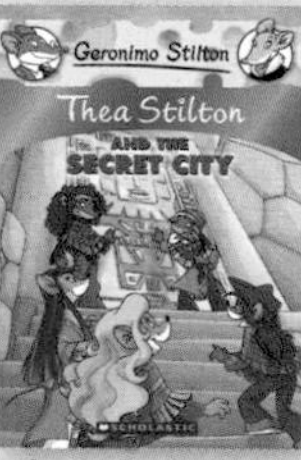

Thea Stilton and the Secret City

Thea Stilton and the Mystery in Paris

Thea Stilton and the Cherry Blossom Adventure

Thea Stilton and the Star Castaways

Thea Stilton: Big Trouble in the Big Apple

Thea Stilton and the Ice Treasure

Thea Stilton and the Secret of the Old Castle

Thea Stilton and the Blue Scarab Hunt

Thea Stilton and the Prince's Emerald

Thea Stilton and the Mystery on the Orient Express

Thea Stilton and the Dancing Shadows

Thea Stilton and the Legend of the Fire Flowers

Thea Stilton and the Spanish Dance Mission

Thea Stilton and the Journey to the Lion's Den

Thea Stilton and the Great Tulip Heist

Thea Stilton and the Chocolate Sabotage

Thea Stilton and the Missing Myth

Thea Stilton and the Lost Letters

Thea Stilton and the Tropical Treasure

Thea Stilton and the Hollywood Hoax

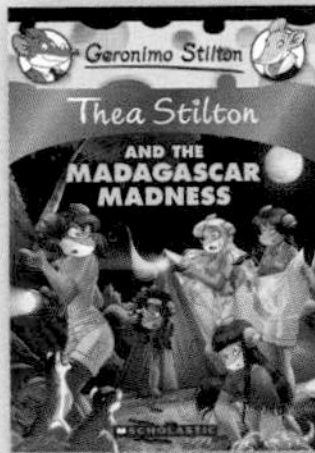

Thea Stilton and the Madagascar Madness

Thea Stilton and the Frozen Fiasco

Thea Stilton and the Venice Masquerade

Thea Stilton and the Niagara Splash

Thea Stilton and the Riddle of the Ruins

Don't miss any of my fabumouse special editions!

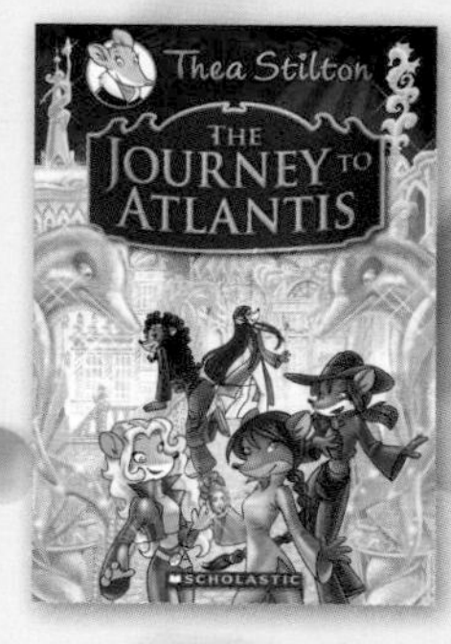

THE JOURNEY TO ATLANTIS

THE SECRET OF THE FAIRIES

THE SECRET OF THE SNOW

THE CLOUD CASTLE

THE TREASURE OF THE SEA

THE LAND OF FLOWERS

THE SECRET OF THE CRYSTAL FAIRIES